Merry Christmas Eve Eve

Jennifer Nice

First published in Great Britain in 2021 by
Write Into The Woods Publishing.

ISBN 978-1-912903-34-4

Cover design and typesetting by Write into the Woods.

www.writeintothewoods.com
www.nicebycandlelight.co.uk

Other Books By Jennifer Nice

Merry Christmas Eve Eve
That's It In A Nutcracker
All's Fair In Love And Christmas

The Idea Of You

Find them all at
www.nicebycandlelight.co.uk

One

'What's the point of fruit cake?' asked Eve, leaning against the wall in the pristine professional kitchen of the Flour Power Bakery.

'One of your five a day,' said Beth. 'Technically, it's healthy.'

'Well…' said Eve. 'If you're going to throw logic at me then this is an argument I can't win.'

Beth grinned as she finished rolling out the white icing for the last Christmas cake.

'Make yourself useful,' she said. 'Start mixing some icing for the cupcakes. They'll be ready soon.' She caught sight of Eve's expression and pointed a finger at her friend. 'No! No eating anything.'

Eve laughed and went to fetch the ingredients. She followed Beth's instructions, putting the icing sugar and butter into the mixer and then they both jumped back as Eve turned the mixer on. A cloud of icing sugar erupted from the bowl and Eve danced and twirled in the cloud.

'Now it's Christmas!'

Beth laughed. Her hair was long and dark, matching her long eyelashes over her chocolate brown eyes. As she spent so much time in her professional kitchen, she nearly always had her hair tied tightly back in a low ponytail or, as today, hidden beneath a flour coated baseball cap.

'Really? Now it's Christmas? I would have thought you'd save that for the chocolate yule log waiting for you in the fridge.'

Eve stopped twirling and stared at her friend.

'Please don't be joking.'

'Would I joke about such a thing? Just promise me you won't eat it all at once. Savour it.'

'Of course. I always savour everything you make.'

'That's true. It does take you ages to eat even the wedding cake tasters I make.'

'Well, that's your own fault. They melt in the mouth.' Eve opened one of the kitchen's large fridges that dominated the back wall and stared open-mouthed at the five chocolate yule logs waiting in there. 'Well, I don't know what to say. You didn't have to make me five.'

'Oh, good. I can spare four for the shop, then?' Beth teased.

Eve shrugged.

'I suppose so. Would hate for you to go out of business.'

Grinning, Beth beckoned for Eve to return to the mixer.

'Pay attention to what you're doing.'

'Sorry, Chef.' Eve returned to watch the icing turn over and over. The twinkling sound of Carol of the Bells began playing and Eve apologised, taking out her phone. She frowned at the name on the screen.

'Who is it?' asked Beth.

'No idea.' Eve answered the phone, holding it up to her ear. 'Hello?'

'Hello, is this a Miss Dutton?'

2

'Speaking.'

'My name's Jeff Hargreaves, Stanley Hargreaves is… was…my father.'

Eve held her breath and then, blinking as her eyes grew hot, she murmured, 'Was?'

The man on the end of the phone sighed.

'My father passed away two nights ago.'

Eve's knees weakened and she groped for something to sit on. Beth, watching her, grabbed a chair from the corner of the room and Eve plonked onto it.

'How?' she murmured.

'His heart just stopped.' Jeff's voice had grown weak and soft but Eve's mind was racing too fast to acknowledge it.

'I'm sorry,' was all she could manage. 'I saw him four days ago,' she added. 'He was his usual self.'

'I understand he had a couple of events booked with you?' Jeff continued.

'Erm. Yeah. A ghost tour and a murder mystery. One for Christmas and one for New Year.' Eve found the words on autopilot, the organised part of her brain clicking into action.

'I'm afraid we'll need to cancel.'

Eve blinked.

'Oh…I…Right.' She searched hard for the right words as her mind span. Cancelling would cost her money, not just in lost expenses but in lost income. What about the people who had bought tickets? The people who were looking forward to the events? But, on the other hand, Stanley Hargreaves had passed away. She could hardly hold the events without him and so soon after his death, especially in his own home. 'No. Of course. Okay.' A single tear dropped down her cheek as her vision blurred.

Beth had turned the mixer off and was watching her friend, her fingers playing at her apron.

'Thank you for understanding,' said Jeff.

'It's just that,' Eve added quickly. 'Everything's booked.

The actors are booked. I'll still need to pay them. And the ghost tour is tomorrow evening. It's a tradition. Stan, erm, Mr Hargreaves always insisted.'

'Okay. But…Look, we're going through his estate now. Everything's in upheaval. There's no time for any events. And really? A ghost tour and a murder mystery?'

'Yeah, no, I understand, but your father loved those events. It's why he let me use the house for free.' Eve snapped her mouth shut as Beth's eyes widened.

'Free?' came Jeff's voice.

Eve scrunched her eyes shut. She shouldn't have said that.

'Well, it was his house,' she answered feebly.

'Right.'

There was an awkward silence.

'So, you'll cancel the events,' said Jeff eventually.

Eve looked up at Beth imploringly, as if her friend had any idea as to what was going on.

'But…it's Christmas,' she said softly.

'Yes, Miss Dutton. And I'm facing my first Christmas without my father.' Jeff's voice broke a little at that and Eve silently scolded herself. 'I'm afraid the events must be cancelled. Thank you.' He hung up without waiting for her reply.

Slowly, Eve lowered her phone and stared up at Beth.

'What's happened?' her friend asked.

Eve couldn't hold back any longer. She promptly burst into tears and shook her head apologetically, excusing herself with a hand gesture and disappearing into the little staff toilet at the back of Beth's bakery.

When she returned, her eyes still red but the sobs quietened, she sat back in the chair and put her head in her hands.

'Stan died two nights ago,' she said quietly.

'Oh, love.' Beth was by her side in a second, wrapping her arms around Eve. 'I'm so sorry.'

Eve hugged her back.

'That was his son on the phone. He says the Christmas events are cancelled.'

Beth frowned and went to argue but then softened.

'Well, I guess it's probably poor taste to run a ghost tour and murder mystery in Stan's house days after he's died.'

Eve nodded.

'Yeah.'

'And the man has just lost his dad.'

'Yeah.' Eve sniffed.

Beth squeezed her.

'It'll be okay. It's just one small business set back. You wouldn't feel able to run those events without Stan, anyway, would you?'

Eve began to shake and Beth pulled away.

'Hang on.' She made her way over to the fridge. 'You need something for the shock.'

'You're not bringing me eggnog, are you?' Eve said, smiling despite herself.

Beth grinned.

'I was wondering if we had any brandy left. Ah, here we go.' She pulled out a small bottle from beside the fridge and opened it, pouring a splash into a measuring cup and handing it to Eve. 'It'll make you feel better,' she urged.

Eve sipped at the brandy and pulled a face, then she downed the lot in one go. Her throat and stomach burned, the heat rushing through her and within seconds, she did feel better.

'Poor Stan,' she murmured.

'How did it happen?' Beth asked, leaning against the fridge and crossing her arms.

'He said his heart just gave out.'

'Well, he was old.'

'Ninety-two.'

'Blimey. And he had a really good life.'

Eve smiled.

'Yeah. He was full of life. He always had a story to tell and he always wanted to be moving, even when he couldn't move far himself. That's why he loved the events, that's why he let me hold them there for free. Oh, Beth.' Eve looked up at her friend. 'What am I going to do? It's not just these two events, is it. I've lost my venue, haven't I. No more ghost tours or murder mysteries at the Manor. Ever. I haven't just lost Stan. What if I lose my business?' Fresh, hot tears were building in Eve's eyes.

'Nope. You always said to me that when life throws you a blockade, you adapt and build around it. Remember?' said Beth. 'Remember when that wedding cake shop opened across the road? Remember what you told me to do?'

'I told you to specialise and go big.'

'You did. And what did I do?'

'You went big and managed to get double spread features in a load of big wedding magazines.'

'And what happened?'

'You survived.' Eve sighed.

'And?'

Eve looked up at Beth, blinking back the tears. 'And?' she asked.

'And my revenue went through the roof. I bought my flat that year, remember?'

Eve looked down at her lap.

'Oh, yeah.'

'So, Stan passing away has put a blockade in your business. What are you going to do once you've grieved for your friend?'

Eve sighed and sat back, looking at the empty measuring cup in her hand.

'Win the lottery and buy the Manor house off his family?'

Beth hesitated.

'I mean…I suppose I was thinking of something that didn't involve winning the lottery.'

'It would be nice, though, wouldn't it. If the house was mine.'

'Well, yeah… You know,' said Beth thoughtfully. 'Stan

loved you. Maybe he's left you something. Some money or something. Heaven knows the man was loaded. Something that you could invest into the business to help you through this.'

Eve frowned. As helpful as that would be, she didn't like the idea of relying on him having left her money. He wasn't a relative, he wasn't part of the business, he'd just been a dear friend who loved socialising and chatting and watching people have fun.

'Maybe. But I doubt it,' she said carefully.

'Well, I guess you can't rely on it,' Beth mused.

Eve sighed and ran her hand over her damp face.

'I'm going to have to let all of those people down. Both events had sold out.' She groaned and held out the measuring cup as Beth offered her more brandy. She sipped at it this time and wiggled her toes in her boots. 'If they put the house on the market, maybe I could look into buying it. It'd be a great investment. I could hold all sort of events there and you could open a little café there. Just think.'

Beth didn't reply and when Eve looked up at her, her friend was giving her a look.

'Yeah. I know. I could never afford it.' Then Eve's eyes brightened. 'We could afford it together? What if we buy it together?'

'You don't even know if they'll sell it,' said Beth. 'Why would they? Stan told you it's been in the family for generations, didn't he? How many kids does he have?'

'Three or four.'

'Right, so they won't sell it. They might argue over it. He's probably left it to them.'

'Maybe whoever gets it would be open to using it as an event space.'

'Eve.' Beth crouched down in front of her friend and waited until she had Eve's full attention. 'Stop thinking. Let it go. At least until after Christmas. They just lost their dad. And you just lost a good friend. Okay? Go and cancel the events, take the hit, and if you like and you need the

7

money, I can swing you a couple of shifts here. We'll be rushed off our feet, so any extra help would be great. If nothing else, it'll take your mind off it. Then, in the New Year, we can start looking for a new venue. A better venue. How about that?'

Eve nodded. Beth was right. Of course, she was right, and with that admission, Eve's chest began to ache. New tears built in her eyes but she blinked them back and sniffed.

'Right. No, you're right. Okay. I'll go cancel on everyone. You're right.' Eve stood and handed Beth the measuring cup just as Carol of the Bells began playing again. Numb, Eve took out her phone and recognised the number that had rung before. 'It's Stan's son again.'

'Answer it. Maybe he's changed his mind,' said Beth.

Two

'Hello?' Eve answered her phone.

'Hi. It's Jeff Hargreaves again. Sorry. We just found some strange stuff in a cupboard. I'm guessing it's something to do with the events you hold here?'

Eve clenched her eyes shut, picturing exactly what he was talking about.

'Yeah. Yes, those are the event props.' Eve pinched the space between her eyes.

'Interesting,' said Jeff. 'When can you come and get them?'

Something in Eve's chest twisted.

'Oh. It's just…Maybe we could talk about the events? I mean, obviously I'll cancel the two coming up, but after that…' Eve drifted off, hoping Jeff would fill in the gaps.

'No. I'm afraid you won't be able to hold any more of these things here. Sorry,' he added as an afterthought, which was something.

Eve swallowed hard to stop herself from crying again.

'Well, maybe it's something we could discuss after Christmas?' she attempted.

'Look. I know my dad loved these things, he loved all of those types of things. But we just can't feasibly do it anymore. I've got enough going on right now, all right? I don't need someone begging me to hold a stupid murder mystery in my family's home at Christmas when my dad's just…' Jeff sighed into the phone and Eve bit her lip, the tears filling her eyes.

She sniffed loudly and nodded as she gulped down a sob.

'Right. No. Of course.' There was a quiver in her voice that she just couldn't hide. 'Just…Stan really did love these things,' she murmured pitifully.

'Dad loved lots of silly things,' said Jeff. 'When can you come and collect it all?'

The second remark about her business being anything but serious was the one that found its way inside Eve. It wiggled and buried itself, and with another sniff, some anger was released.

'Well, bah humbug to you too. I'll come now, shall I? Get this all over with so you can be rid of me.' Eve hung up without letting Jeff respond and then instantly regretted it. She closed her eyes and took a deep breath. The poor man had just lost his father and she was screaming "bah humbug" at him. What did that make her?

She blinked back another wave of tears. She didn't deserve them, she didn't deserve to feel sorry for herself.

Eve wandered back into the kitchen where Beth was carefully trimming the icing from the cake. She stopped as Eve appeared and plonked herself back onto the chair.

'Got any more alcohol?'

'Why? What did he say? What happened?'

'I'm an idiot, Beth,' Eve murmured. 'I called him a bah humbug.'

Beth smothered a smirk.

'Oh, Eve.'

'He's found the props Stan let me stash at the house. I have to go pick them up.'

'When? Do you want me to come with you?'

'No. That's okay. It won't take long and I'll have more room in the car if it's just me. I can fill up the passenger seat. And anyway, you've got a thriving business to run.'

Beth sighed.

'So have you,' she said, wrapping her arms around Eve and giving her a tight hug. 'But let yourself feel first, okay? Go get your stuff, say goodbye to the house, grieve, eat Christmas food and then we'll sit down and figure out your next steps. Together. All right?'

Eve nodded, still fighting the tears as she hung onto Beth's arms. She mentally shook herself and fetched her coat and bag.

'All right. Here we go. Now or never. Or later, I guess. But now it is. I'll call you later?'

'Definitely,' said Beth, returning to her cake. 'Be careful driving.'

Eve left the bakery, weaving around the tables of couples, friends and families all chatting and sliding their forks through soft cakes, sipping at coffees. She passed the steamed up windows, delicately decorated with festive stickers, and out onto the cold December high street. The door shut behind her and the sound of happy chatter and scent of coffee left her. Eve paused for a moment on the pavement while she wrapped her scarf around her chin and lips. There was a heavy chill in the air that forced her eyes to the sky and the ominous grey clouds that had to be heavy with snow.

Eve hadn't checked the weather recently and it was a shock to see those clouds. Perhaps it was no bad thing that she would have to cancel the events once she was home. The tears sprang forth then. Stan would have loved the snow. She would have driven up the long driveway to the manor house and he would have been waiting, standing on the porch, in a bobble hat and tightly wrapped scarf but with his coat undone, excited to see the first flakes fall. Janine, his housekeeper of thirty years, would have appeared behind him, chastising him for going outside without his coat done up properly, and Stan would have challenged her, a big grin on his face, that he was indeed still technically inside the house, being under the shelter of the porch.

Eve smiled.

She would miss that big grin of his and the way it lit up his eyes, grown light with age but still twinkling whenever he was excited or happy. Eve tried to remember other things about him, bringing to mind anything vivid, as she walked to her car and dug around in her bag for her keys.

Quite a few things made his eyes twinkle. Whenever she'd brought cakes from Beth's shop for him to taste, when the leaves started to change in autumn, at the first sign of the daffodils poking through the soil in spring, at the request of a story from his youth, whenever he talked about his children and wife. Christmas, however, excited Stan more than anything else.

Eve frowned as she started the ignition, trying to remember their conversations about Stan's family. He'd lost his wife fifteen years earlier after a long illness. His voice had broken every time he mentioned her, and each time it caught at Eve's heart, as the memory did now.

Did he have three children or four? There were two boys, she remembered that much. The eldest and the youngest were his sons, but were there one or two daughters in the middle? Eve didn't know their names or which son Jeff was. Stan had spoken of all of them highly, with great pride and love, so it had always been quite hard to tell them apart. The eldest was divorced and the youngest had never married, she remembered that much. Stan wasn't a fan of his daughter's husband. Last time they'd spoken of it, he'd been gossiping that something wasn't right in the relationship and that perhaps it was nearing the end. He'd been hoping for a divorce by Christmas. Eve hadn't given an opinion on the topic, not knowing the people involved, but it had seemed a little mean of Stan to want something like that for his daughter. And what of the other daughter? Was she happily married or did she not exist? Eve laughed despite herself, as if that's all there was in life. To be happily married or to not exist. Stan had certainly not believed that. He'd talked for hours about how proud he was of his children's careers and families. As long as they were happy, he'd always say, then he was happy.

Eve drove through the town, reaching the edge and passing into the countryside. There was something peaceful about having open fields on either side, even as the road narrowed. She knew these roads so well, having held events at Stan's house for a few years. She'd been the one to approach him. Within weeks of starting her events business, she'd been scouting venues and had driven past the Manor. It was stunning and Gothic-looking, perfect for a murder mystery. She'd immediately driven home to research the property and discovered a ghost story set in the grounds. If it hadn't been for that, she probably would never have thought about holding ghost tours. The next day, before she lost her nerve, she'd driven back to the Manor, up the imposing driveway and knocked on the door. Janine had answered and, knowing her employer well, had disappeared into the house to mention it to Stan. Eve had expected to be told he'd call her back, only to never hear from him, so she'd been shocked in the best of ways when Stan had appeared at the door and invited her in for a tour. From the beginning, he'd been warm, friendly and thrilled to hear all of her ideas. She'd asked him for a venue hire quote then but he wouldn't hear of it. Instead, he'd offered her a deal. She could hold the events in the house for free, as long as nothing was broken or damaged of course, and in return, he would be able to attend and take part in every single event.

Eve couldn't have agreed any faster.

Stan had always been fun-loving. He just wanted his last years to be filled with laughter and joy, and that had become his mission. Sure, he'd slowed down since Eve had first met him, and sometimes he coughed after laughing. He'd had to start sitting more often and watching the events from afar rather than being directly involved. That was why she'd started running more murder mysteries, held in the grand sitting room with a roaring fire. It was also why Stan had started placing gadgets around the house whenever there was a ghost tour, so that wherever he was, unable to join in, he would be able to hear their gasps and yelps of fear and surprise. Eve and Janine had both worked hard to convince him to keep those frights to a minimum, and only let him do exactly what he wanted on the Halloween tours.

Christmas is about gentle spirits, Eve had often told him when it came time for the Christmas ghost tour. Think the Ghosts of Christmas Past, Present and Future rather than the Woman in Black.

Stan had reluctantly agreed and then earlier that year had hired a local girl on her black horse to ride through the Manor's grounds while wearing a long black cloak. It had led to screaming and one woman feeling faint, especially when the sound of a rocking chair came through the ceiling from the attic above. Eve had almost worried until every single customer on the tour claimed they would be returning the following year.

Well, that wouldn't be happening now.

Eve wondered then if she'd ever hold another ghost tour. They'd been Stan's favourite event and she'd only had the idea because of his house. Somehow, it didn't seem quite right to run them without him. They wouldn't be as good, for one thing, without his ideas.

Eve turned into the driveway of the Manor and drove towards the large house with its three floors and Gothic edges. The tall trees on either side of the driveway were bare, save for the twinkling lights wrapped around each trunk, giving an excellent view of the gardens in dull greens and browns, sleeping through the winter. Eve sighed. What would happen to the gardens now that Stan wasn't there to hand them over to the two retired gentlemen from the town who busied themselves there all summer? The gardens had been their project once they'd left their office jobs and Stan had pretty much let them do whatever they wanted. Small hedges and beautifully pruned shrubs had popped up along with glorious flower beds of bright colours, pathways of short lush grass leading around them, to a small orchard of apple and pear trees. That orchard had come in handy for the ghost tours, where the group would stop for one of Beth's toffee apples or a freshly baked mince pie.

Something in Eve gave way as she parked up outside the house, next to a large Land Rover and a smaller, sleek BMW.

Three

Eve tapped the top of her steering wheel. She didn't want to get out of the car. To get out and knock on the door would be to confirm that Stan wouldn't be answering. Instead, she stayed in her car a moment longer, looking out over the gardens and up at the house, trying hard to memorise every tiny detail about them. The clouds were becoming heavier, if that was possible, and a chill ran through Eve as the car cooled down. With another deep sigh, she got out, tightened her scarf and coat around her and headed for the porch. Stan always decorated, or rather directed Janine how to decorate, the house at the beginning of December, and nothing had changed about the decorations since Eve's last visit to the house four days ago. There was a sprig of mistletoe hanging over the door under the porch. Every Christmas, Stan planted a crafty kiss on every woman's cheek who happened to pass through the front door. There was also greenery and holly around the wooden beams, probably taken from the gardens at the back.

Eve choked back a sob as she stepped onto the doorstep and rang the bell. The sound echoed through the house and she listened with her eyes closed, her chest tightening as she waited for someone who wasn't Stan to open the door.

The sound of the latch being lifted and the lock being turned made her slowly open her eyes and look up at the man standing in the doorway. His hair was a soft light brown and grown a little too long in her opinion. It was close to flopping in his eyes and meant that he had to keep sweeping his hand through it to push it back. His eyes were blue and hard, staring down at her as he frowned, etching lines into his forehead and the corner of his eyes. It was an expression that was so far away from Stan's beaming grin that Eve couldn't stop the tears falling down her cheeks.

'I'm here to collect my props,' she managed to say, her voice cracking. The man didn't move at first and when he did, it was to lean forward and look up at the sky. Confused, Eve followed his gaze and then looked back to him.

'Is it snowing?' he asked.

'Not yet,' she told him. 'Looks like it will.'

'Is that fake snow?'

'What?'

'In your hair.' He gestured at her face and Eve's eyes widened.

'Oh.' She pulled a hand through her hair and then, as the man looked on disgusted, she tasted what was on her fingers. 'It's icing sugar,' she said, a smile twitching at her lips. Stan would have laughed, *Been dancing in the kitchen again, have we?*

This man didn't ask that, but the frown had turned into something softer and more curious.

'My friend owns a bakery,' she explained. 'I was helping to make icing when…' Her smile fell. 'When I got the call about…'

The man's expression also fell.

'You're Eve Dutton? Jeff Hargreaves.' He held out a

17

hand which Eve found strange, although she took it without thinking. They shook and then Jeff seemed to realise what he'd done. He took his warm hand back a little too quickly and actually gave his head a little shake. She watched him, her hand still warm from his.

'Come in,' he told her, moving aside.

Eve took a step forward and then stopped before taking a few steps back.

'What are you doing?'

'Hang on,' she said, flipping her hair over her head and giving it a ruffle with her hands. It wasn't as long as Beth's but hung just below her shoulders and when Eve was feeling generous she would call it a caramel brown. It still did a good flick, the icing sugar dropping in front of her in a small cloud. When she flicked her hair back, she smoothed it down and caught Jeff with a surprised look on his face. 'Don't want to leave icing sugar in the house,' she told him before doing a double take at his eyes. Now that they'd softened, even a little, there was something about them. Something familiar. Eve smiled as Jeff led her into the house. They may have been brighter with youth, but Jeff had his father's eyes.

Eve stopped in the middle of the large square hallway. In the corner was the impressive staircase leading around the wall and up to the first floor with its decadent red carpet and sparkling gold trim. The polished oak panelling, which led to a sitting room on the right, an office space on the left and the kitchen straight ahead, was glistening in the twinkling fairy lights that adorned the tall Christmas tree. The tree was where it always was, although this one was taller than last year's. Positioned in the corner of the staircase so that you could stand on the stairs to decorate it, the tree was festooned with glass baubles, toy trinkets and sparkling trails of gold. On the top, an angel was awkwardly perched looking like she'd much rather be where there wasn't the top of a tree poking up her skirt.

Eve stared up at the angel, her eyes aching as she

remembered watching Stan standing on the stairs, carefully placing the angel on top of the tree while apologising to it. She swallowed a sob down, making her chest ache.

'Dad always liked to decorate early. It's been this way since the first of December. He sent me a photo of the tree once it was up,' came Jeff's voice from behind her. He was staring up at the tree too, although Eve didn't dare look at him properly. She tried to wipe her eyes on her sleeve without him noticing but failed.

'I always decorate on the first too,' she said, trying to keep her voice level. 'I was always jealous of how much space Stan has…had. I always dreamed of having a tree this big.'

From the corner of her eye, she could see Jeff looking at her.

'Yes. Well. Your stuff is over here. I found it in a cupboard.'

'I'm surprised you're going through everything so soon,' said Eve, following Jeff further into the hallway. Everything in this house seemed large, even the cupboards and what Stan referred to as "cosy nooks".

'Oh, it's all the legal stuff. Dad left a will but there's inheritance tax and a load of other stuff I don't really understand. I tend to leave that to my sister. She's a solicitor. It's her firm dealing with it all.'

Eve nodded.

'I wouldn't understand all that stuff either,' she told him. He gave her a small smile and opened the cupboard door.

'To be honest, I thought this was all Dad's until I saw your name on some of it.'

'Yeah. Stan bought some of his own so we needed to know what belonged to who.' Eve reached out and pulled on the flap of a cardboard box full of costumes. Eve's name was scrawled on the side. She frowned. That was new. She ran her fingers over her name.

'I didn't know he'd done this. This wasn't here before.'

She looked up at Jeff. 'Did he know he was…' she drifted off, unable to finish the sentence. Jeff's features softened further and he became more familiar. There was something about his lips and the twitch of his mouth. She'd seen it before.

'He'd been ill for a while. You didn't know?'

Eve's stomach twisted with a sickening lurch.

'No. Why wouldn't he tell me,' she murmured. 'What was wrong?'

'His heart,' said Jeff. 'He had a heart attack when he was in his eighties. I always thought he did really well after that, considering. We had to force him to slow down, but now I realise that he didn't slow down as much as I would have liked.' He turned to look over the contents of the cupboard. Eve followed his gaze.

'But it made him happy,' she said softly.

Jeff's eyes returned to her and she slowly turned to meet them.

'He mentioned you, you know.'

Eve blinked. She hadn't been expecting that.

'Really? What did he say?'

'Don't worry, it was all good things. He didn't mention the events, just said a nice young woman called Eve often dropped by with treats. I worried for a moment until he reassured me that he meant cakes.'

Eve almost laughed.

'From your friend's bakery, I assume?' Jeff continued.

'She makes the best,' Eve told him.

'I had to tell him off. Cake isn't…wasn't good for his heart.'

'He never told me about the heart attack. Otherwise I would have been more careful,' Eve assured him, although she questioned the statement as soon as it left her mouth. If she gave it proper thought and allowed for Stan's inevitable argument, she still would have brought the cakes round. He was over ninety and he'd earned them. That's what he would have said and she'd have been inclined to agree.

'When was the last time you saw him?' asked Jeff.

Eve sighed, pulling out a wide-brimmed hat with a large feather from the cupboard and putting it on without thinking. Jeff smiled at her although it came with confusion.

'Only four days ago, although it seems like a long time now. We met to go over arrangements for the Christmas events. The last event before these was on Halloween. We always did a ghost tour and Stan ended up turning it into a haunted house event that ended in the orchard.' Eve smiled at the memories. 'Stan made it more fun than I ever could have. And my friend provided toffee apples and Stan's friends arranged apple bobbing. It wouldn't have been much without them. I just had the basic idea and hired the medium.'

'Medium?'

'To do the tour. She takes everyone round the house seeing if she can sense ghosts.'

Jeff raised an eyebrow.

'You don't really believe in ghosts, do you?'

'What does that matter?' Eve asked, swapping her hat for another, this time a small Victorian bowler hat.

'I mean, you don't believe she can sense ghosts?'

'I don't know. Did you know that it's illegal to claim that she can? Sort of. She fully believes that she can sense and talk to ghosts but legally she has to call herself an actor and say it's all for entertainment purposes. Do you know why?'

'Why?' asked Jeff, glancing up at the bowler hat on Eve's head.

'Because otherwise she's breaking a law that originated as the Witchcraft Act. Isn't that great? Basically, if she claims it's all real then she's a witch in the eyes of the law. In a roundabout sort of way.'

Jeff held her gaze for a little too long. Eve wilted a little. His eyes were too bright and too blue and she was pretty sure that she just saw a twinkle. She looked away quickly, taking off the bowler hat and replacing it with a cowboy hat.

'I always liked that fact,' she added and stopped rifling through the cupboard to stare into empty space. 'Yeah. Four days ago. Not even a week. I brought mince pies and we ate them around the fire in the sitting room while we made plans.'

Jeff stood silently beside her, perhaps lost in his own memories and regrets.

'He liked you,' he murmured. 'A lot. You brought a lot of fun into his life and I guess that had more to do with these events than the cakes. So…thank you.'

Eve turned to look Jeff in the eye.

'I owe your father so much,' she said gently, aware of a new wave of tears building. 'So, emptying the cupboard,' she added as Jeff's eyes softened again. She turned back to the boxes and started to pull bits and pieces out.

'Yes. I'll help. Is it all going in your car? Will it fit?'

'Should do,' said Eve, filling her arms with a bag of ghostly decorations and placing the bowler hat on top of the cowboy hat already on her head. 'Fill up the car and then when I get it all home, I need to cancel the events.'

'You haven't done that yet?'

'I haven't exactly had time to sit down with a list of names yet.'

'But isn't it tomorrow?'

Eve stopped and turned back to Jeff, precariously balancing the hats above her.

'Yes.'

'So…shouldn't you have cancelled it immediately?'

'You mean immediately after you told me Stan had passed away while I was sobbing my eyes out in my friend's kitchen or immediately after you told me to come and empty the cupboard?'

Jeff hesitated.

'Won't they be angry at the short notice?'

Eve shrugged and then dropped the bag of decorations as she reached out to stop the bowler hat falling off.

'I'm sure they'll understand when I tell them about Stan. They can't really argue that, can they.'

'No. I guess not. And you'll have to refund them all.'

'Of course,' said Eve, picking up the bag of decorations while trying to keep her head straight and the hats balanced.

'So, you'll be out of pocket.'

'I did mention that, didn't I?'

Jeff watched Eve as she slowly turned back towards the front door.

'What if we held the ghost tour?' he said.

Eve stopped and gently turned back.

'Excuse me?' she said, stepping towards him, wondering if she'd heard right or if the hats on her head had somehow muffled the words.

'What's going on here?' came a deep voice. Jeff and Eve both turned to the man who had spoken and both the bowler hat and cowboy hat fell off Eve's head, bouncing on the parquet flooring.

Four

The man watched the bowler hat roll for a moment before it settled on the polished floor, then he looked up at Eve. She gave him a quick smile and then tried to dive for the door.

'This is Eve Dutton,' said Jeff. 'She's the one who runs the events Dad used to have here. She's just here to collect her stuff. This is Glen, my brother,' Jeff told Eve.

Eve, struggling with the bag of decorations in her arms, gave Glen another smile and a nod. He looked her up and down, his gaze landing on the bag.

'What stuff? She was keeping stuff here?'

'She's in the room,' Eve muttered before trying to open the front door without any free hands. She sighed and looked back to Jeff for help.

'Props. For the events,' said Jeff, picking up the hats.

'What sort of events need props?'

'A murder mystery,' Eve told Glen. He raised an eye-brow at her. 'Everyone's encouraged to take on the role of a character. Stan would usually sit in the corner and watch so we created a character for him.'

'Let me guess, he'd be the elderly, wealthy man being used for his house and not getting paid?'

Eve reeled, rocking back on her heels and blinking at the force of Glen's anger. She opened her mouth to speak but the words wouldn't come. Thankfully, Jeff managed to find the right thing to say.

'Oh, come on, Glen. Dad would have loved it. You know that.' Jeff reached around Eve and opened the door for her. Thanking him quietly, she walked through and dumped the bag of decorations by her car. Glen and Jeff stayed inside the house so she returned, keeping her head down, meaning to retrieve the hats from Jeff.

To her surprise, he had put the bowler hat on despite being seemingly in a deep conversation, or perhaps argument, with his brother. Eve stopped. There was something almost handsome about Jeff Hargreaves in a bowler hat, although handsome wasn't something that Eve generally liked. She preferred quirky and fun, in both her friends and the men she let into her life. Stan had been quirky and fun. The smile faded from her face at the memory of his grin as he'd put on the flat cap that was currently still in the box in the cupboard. He'd take the cap and an elegant silver-topped walking cane and sit in the corner, leaning forward, taking part as much as he could even as the warm fire attempted to lull anyone who'd had more than one drink to sleep.

'You need to grow up,' Glen was saying.

'And you need to relax,' Jeff retorted. He bit his lip and sighed as Glen's eyes became noticeably watery. 'I'm sorry. I didn't mean that.'

Glen shook his head and rubbed at his eyes. Something inside Eve shifted.

'How can you wear that thing right now?' Glen murmured, glancing at the bowler hat.

Slowly, Jeff took it off and handed it to Eve. She

muttered an apology, taking the hat and darting around the men, back to the cupboard.

'Here you both are,' came a woman's voice. When Eve walked back through carrying the box of hats, there was a woman with hair the same colour as Jeff's and eyes the same as Glen's. She stopped when she saw Eve and Jeff once again explained what was going on as Eve dodged around them and outside to her car.

When she re-entered the house, she stopped and sighed, preparing herself.

'I'm so sorry, about your father. Stan was an amazing man,' she told them. 'I didn't know him for that long, really, but some of my favourite memories from the last few years are of being in this house, and your father had some incredible ideas.'

'That was Dad,' the woman murmured, glancing at Jeff. 'This is my sister, Wendy.'

Eve gave Wendy a smile which Wendy did her best to return. She was a tall woman with long flowing hair and there was something equally intimidating and friendly about her. Eve wasn't sure whether to relax around her or be cautious. She was just about to skirt around the group to return to the cupboard and avoid having to decide how to act when Wendy spoke.

'Dad did like his fun.' She looked appraisingly at Eve. 'And you just ran events here?'

Eve may not have known how to take Wendy, but she knew she didn't like that tone. She narrowed her eyes at Wendy and reminded herself that the woman had just lost her father.

'Stan was always kind and respectful to me, and generous. We had a business arrangement, that I could use his house as a venue but only if he could take part in each event. For which I am truly grateful, because his ideas made the events better. I know he only gave me the ideas so he could have more fun.'

Wendy pursed her lips and then shrugged, turning to

her brothers.

'Won't you be lonely here, Jeff? It's a very large house for one man. I was always telling Dad that. Maybe you should stay in your London flat.'

Realising she'd been dismissed, Eve wandered slowly around the siblings and back to the cupboard, pricking her ears as she went.

'If you're about to suggest we sell this place, you can forget it,' came Glen's voice as Eve reached the cupboard. She stopped and stared at the remaining few boxes, not moving. 'It's staying in the family. That's what Dad wanted and it'll be in his will.'

'Of course I'm not suggesting we sell it,' Wendy snapped. 'I'm saying that Jeff can't fill it.'

'Oh, thanks. You don't see me having children and dogs to fill it?'

'You don't even have a girlfriend, so when are you planning on having these children?'

There was a snort which Eve assumed was Jeff.

'Let me guess, you want the house?'

'At least I have children to fill it with voices,' said Wendy.

'You already have your family home.' That was Glen. 'This house was always going to be Jeff's. That's what Dad always said.'

'You know, technically, the eldest should get it,' said Wendy.

'Yeah, well, the eldest is saying that it's Jeff's. End of conversation.' There was a clap, which must have been Glen punctuating the end of his sentence. 'And as I said, it'll be in Dad's will, so there's no argument to have.'

'Fine. But you're not doing what Dad did and running a business from this place. This is our family home,' said Wendy.

'Of course not.' Although Jeff's voice had lost some of its power. Eve held her breath, willing him to say more. She exhaled in a puff when he appeared beside her, giving her a strange look, and then testing the weight of the nearest box.

'Everything okay?' he asked.

Eve nodded.

'You were saying,' she murmured. 'About holding the last ghost tour?'

Jeff looked into her eyes and Eve's stomach twisted pleasurably. She looked away before she could fully register it, checking inside one of the boxes that she already knew contained costumes. There was something increasingly attractive about Jeff. It was probably the knowledge that he'd be getting the house. She was being vain and shallow. Eve steadied herself. It was just a hint of envy, morphing into an attraction for the wealthy, single man beside her who had what she wanted. That was all. It didn't mean anything.

'Yeah. Dad would have liked that, wouldn't he.'

Eve glanced sideways at Jeff. Was he talking to her or himself?

'They're reading his will once all the red tape is dealt with,' he continued.

'Hmm? Oh. Yes,' said Eve, frowning. How was she supposed to respond to that? 'Red tape?' she asked, fumbling for words.

'Yeah. Legal stuff. I don't know. That's Wendy's thing.'

'Right.'

Jeff smiled to himself.

'Do you know why she's called Wendy?'

Eve straightened and gave this some thought. Finally, she turned to Jeff, grinning.

'Because of Peter Pan? Stan always seemed so young at heart.'

'He used to read us Peter Pan when we were little.' Jeff nodded. 'He used to say Glen and I were John and Michael, and Wendy was Wendy. I always used to ask why he called us Glen and Jeff, in that case.'

'Why did he?'

'Mum. She said John was boring and she used to know a Michael. So here we are.'

'I prefer Glen and Jeff,' said Eve.

'Me too. It didn't help my sister's ego though. Being called Wendy just made her think she was special.'

'Well, she was. She's the only girl,' said Eve before remembering that only a couple of hours earlier she'd thought there were two sisters. 'She is, right?'

'Yeah. There's three of us. And Dad will have split everything as fairly as he could, because that's what he always did. Even though he doesn't need to. Not really.'

'No?'

'No. But he always said I'd get the house. I don't know why.'

Eve caught herself studying Jeff's features.

'Because you look like him,' she murmured under her breath. That was why he seemed so familiar. That was why she'd seen that smile before. His features were littered around the house, in photographs of Stan as a young man. Of course, there were also photos of the children, of Glen, Wendy and Jeff when they were little. Yet, comparing the three of them, Jeff's presence was the one that seemed to resonate within the house.

Jeff searched her eyes and then gave a sad smile.

'Mum used to say that.'

'Jeff?'

They both jumped at Glen's voice and then Jeff's brother appeared in the hallway. He was taller than Jeff, and bulkier, with broader shoulders, something of a belly and brown eyes rimmed red with spent tears. He ran a hand through his dark hair and sighed.

'Wendy's finishing up. You nearly done?' He eyed the boxes and then gave Eve a quick glance.

'Just helping Eve put these in her car and I think I'm all sorted.'

'Those events are cancelled?' Glen asked.

Jeff looked back to Eve and then turned to his brother.

Eve silently begged him.

'Yeah,' said Jeff. 'Except the ghost tour. It's tomorrow. It'd be a shame to let those people down.'

Glen struggled for a moment.

'C'mon, Glen,' his brother urged. 'One last hoorah for Dad. Plus, it's Christmas. Can we really disappoint those people at Christmas?'

Glen rolled his eyes but didn't respond. He only sighed again, crossing his arms. It took Eve a second to realise he was hugging himself. His gaze landed back on her and she snapped her eyes back up to his.

'Dad loved the ghost tours?'

She nodded a little too eagerly.

'He always wanted to make them scarier. We had to hold him back, except on Halloween. We let his imagination run wild then. He practically turned this place into a haunted house. But not at Christmas. It's more of a festive event, looking at the Manor's history with some spooky tales. Think less Exorcist and more Scrooge.'

A smile touched Glen's lips.

'And you lead them round?' he asked her.

'Oh no. I just run it all, in the background really. I have a medium, a physic, that I hire to lead the tour. She knows the Manor and the stories well now. And Stan used to help me decorate the house. We end in the orchard. We put fairy lights in the trees and hand out mulled wine and mince pies which my friend makes. She's a baker. We were going to have the brass band from the town over to play some carols too.'

Jeff's eyes widened as she spoke.

'That sounds amazing.' He turned to his brother. 'Dad would have loved that.'

Glen's features had softened.

'He would. But Wendy's right. This is our family home. The idea of people traipsing through it talking about ghosts.' He shuddered. 'Could we just do the orchard bit?'

'They've paid for the ghost tour,' said Eve carefully, her

mind whirring. 'I guess we could. I'd have to give them some sort of refund though.'

'Or offer to donate the money to charity,' Glen offered.

Eve bristled.

'I think Eve was hoping to pay rent and buy food with that money,' Jeff murmured to his brother.

'Oh. Right.' Glen looked into the cupboard at the remaining boxes. 'We'll think about it,' he told her after a moment's consideration.

Eve hesitated.

'So…I shouldn't cancel it?'

'Not yet,' said Glen.

'No. Just the murder mystery,' said Jeff at the same time.

'Okay.' Eve held back the grin that wanted to beam from her. She could do that. She could run just the one event. That would see her through to January without too much harm done, then she could look into sourcing a new venue.

'We just have to discuss it with Wendy first,' said Glen.

'Oh.' Eve sagged, her hopes dissipating before they'd even fully formed.

Five

Eve stopped by the Flour Power Bakery on her way home. Something in the boxes on the back seats rattled as she stopped the car. She slammed the door, locking it behind her as she stepped into the warmth of freshly baked mince pies, hot coffee and friendly chatter. Pausing only to breathe in the aromas, Eve headed straight to the back, saying hello to Pete behind the till as she passed.

'She's in the kitchen,' he called to her. Eve gave him a thumbs up and squeezed past a family crowded around a small table.

'Beth?' Eve entered the kitchen carefully, aware she was bringing her dirty coat and shoes into the food preparation area.

'Eve! How did it go?' Beth appeared, wiping her hands on a towel. She offered Eve an apron but Eve shook her head.

'Sorry. I've got a car full of boxes and bags and I need to go home and cancel things.'

'Oh.' Beth sighed. 'I'm sorry. It didn't go well then?'

Eve leaned against the wall thoughtfully.

'I don't know. Stan's sons seem lovely. All three of his kids were there, and I say kids, they all seem older than us. Jeff told me to just cancel the murder mystery at New Year's but we'll go ahead with the ghost tour.'

'Really? That's great.' Beth grinned and then stopped. 'Isn't that a bit morbid, given that Stan's only just passed away?'

'Jeff said it would be fitting, his dad would have loved it. And he's right.'

Beth raised an eyebrow.

'And how much did it take to convince him?'

'Oh, no. I didn't. Well, not much. Well…I don't think. He seemed to come to the conclusion on his own. I pointed out it was Christmas and the ghost tour is tomorrow and how sad it would be. Then I ended up telling him about the ghost tours we've done in the past and how good Stan made them and here we are. He changed his mind. But I still have to go cancel the murder mystery. And call Lyn to tell her about Stan. For a physic, she's not always good at reading the room.'

Beth scoffed at that.

'I wonder why,' she muttered.

'She's not a fake. She's adamant about that,' said Eve, before adding quietly, 'Do you ever wonder if we think she's a fake because believing in her would be too scary?'

'They're all fake, Eve.'

Eve shot Beth a look but didn't have the energy to replay that argument yet again. She'd need a coffee and a lot of chocolate for that one.

'She's a good actress though. She brings a wonderful theatre to it and that's all that Stan ever really wanted. To really spook people.'

'She's definitely spooky.'

Eve ignored that.

'So,' Beth continued, a smirk growing on her lips as she

reached for her water bottle. 'Stan's sons are nice, are they?'

Eve smiled before realising what she was doing and stopping herself.

'Yeah, well. Stan was nice, so it stands to reason, doesn't it. Glen – he's the eldest – isn't sure about the ghost tour. But all three had a bit of a fight about the house while I was packing up the car and it sounds like the Manor is going to Jeff. Given his turn around on the ghost tour, that might be good news.' Eve bit her lip as her thoughts raced. 'If I can make this ghost tour amazing, show Jeff just how good it can be, maybe he'll let me keep using the Manor as a venue.'

'That shouldn't be too hard,' said Beth.

'Well. It might. Glen and Wendy aren't happy about the house being used for events.'

'Wendy? Is she Glen's wife?'

'No, their sister. Oh, Beth. I'm not sure about her. I know she's just lost her dad, but she didn't seem happy about Jeff getting the house and Jeff's the only one on my side. Even Glen said they'd have to talk to her first about the ghost tour. She's going to say no.' Eve swallowed on the lump rising in her throat.

'Well, she can't, can she. It's already organised and it's tomorrow night.'

'But it's their house. She could just say no tomorrow and I'd be forced to cancel.' Eve sighed. 'I'd have to refund everyone and still pay Lyn and the brass band. That's too short notice.'

Beth pursed her lips.

'Forget about that. Go with your first plan. Make this ghost tour amazing. I've already baked most of the mince pies. I can do cookies as well, if you like? Gingerbread with icing. Gingerbread Christmas ghosts. We could make little goody bags for them to take home.' Beth's eyes were growing distant, as they always did when she got an idea.

'Sounds amazing,' said Eve. 'Do that. If it all goes to pot, then I'll have them all. Tomorrow evening. By myself.

With ice cream and wine.'

Beth gave Eve a look.

'Stop thinking the worst. Go home, get planning and I'll get baking.'

As Eve turned to leave, Beth had a change of heart and asked playfully, 'So, erm, is Jeff or Glen single?'

Eve rolled her eyes.

'Yes. Jeff is. I don't know about Glen. Why? You want me to set you up?'

'It just occurred to me that this Jeff was all about cancelling these events until he set eyes on you. Then suddenly he changes his mind? Come on.'

Eve caught herself smiling as she replayed their first meeting in her mind.

'No. It wasn't like that. He changed his mind after I told him about the efforts his dad used to go to. He's grieving his father, Beth. That stuff has got to be the furthest from his mind right now.'

'Oh, please. My cousin got together with her husband at a funeral. It's what it does to you. It's like you need to feel something life affirming after such a loss. Imagine, if you fell in love, you wouldn't have to worry about using the house as a venue.'

'I still think Wendy would object, even if we were sisters.'

'No, I meant because you wouldn't need to worry about money.'

'Oh. Oh!' Eve glanced around for something to throw at her friend and although there was nothing to hand, Beth giggled and dodged. 'I wouldn't marry someone just for their house and I wouldn't give up my business if I came into money. Would you give up this bakery if you married someone with money?'

'Absolutely not,' said Beth, still giggling. 'But I notice you haven't objected to the idea of marrying Jeff.'

Eve narrowed her eyes at her friend.

'Is he attractive?' Beth asked, forcing away the giggles.

. Eve smiled at her.

'He wouldn't like me.'

'Pfft. Of course he would.'

'I took the hats to the car by piling them on my head.'

Beth stopped giggling and stood still, staring at her friend.

'Oh, Eve. If he didn't fall madly in love with you in that moment then he doesn't deserve you.' Beth snorted. 'Wish I'd seen it.'

'And you didn't tell me I had icing sugar in my hair when I left. Jeff thought it was fake snow.'

Beth laughed.

'That was the first conclusion he came to? You're made for each other.'

The two women grinned at one another and then Eve noticed the tray of mince pies waiting on the side.

'I'm taking one of these. In compensation for you thinking I would marry for money. Just be glad I'm not throwing this at you.' She took a bite of the mince pie, still warm from the oven, and gave a little moan of pleasure. 'These are so good.'

Beth said nothing but she didn't need to, her expression and the light in her eyes said it all.

'See you tomorrow,' said Eve around her mouthful. Beth waved to her and Eve walked back into the main part of the bakery, leaving the sound of Beth's laughter behind her.

Once home, Eve dithered about whether to leave the boxes and bags of murder mystery props and costumes in the car or whether to take them upstairs to her flat. After weighing up her options and testing the weight of one of the boxes, she decided to leave them for the time being, or until she could bribe some friends to help her. Once in her flat, she chucked her keys into the little bowl on the side, slid out of her coat, turned the heating on and did the customary dance to warm up while making cold noises. In the kitchen, she filled the kettle and turned it on, and then Eve stopped.

Her mind swam, from painful jolts in her chest at the memories of Stan and the thought of never seeing him again to wondering what the future held for the event business she loved so much. As her breathing grew shallow, Eve sat on her kitchen floor, hugging her knees to her chest, and she let the tears come. The sobs wracked through her body, her nose running and she let out wails of grief as they washed over her.

Once the crying had subsided and the kettle clicked to say it was boiled, Eve picked herself up and found a box of tissues to clean and dry her face. With a steaming cup of tea and feeling a little lighter, Eve sat on her sofa and pulled her laptop over. She would have to cancel the murder mystery event first, then she would need to call Lyn and Bob, her brass band contact, to update them. In theory, the ghost tour was planned and ready to go, but Eve would double check everything that night. Then, she should go to bed.

That was her plan and it had been a good plan, except that when she finally did fall into bed, after more tears and awkward phone calls and curling up to feel sorry for herself, she just couldn't sleep.

Every time she closed her eyes, they pinged back open and her mind swam from one thought to the next. Soon, her memories of Stan were merging with those of meeting his children earlier that day. His stature merging with Wendy's, his hair with Glen's, his eyes with Jeff's. Eve found herself picking apart the new memories of Jeff, matching his smile and tone to his father's. Eve would miss Stan's laugh, his excitement, his sense of fun, and then her mind pushed the vision of Jeff to her. The man who might give her some hope this Christmas, the man who might give her hope next year, if only she could impress him enough with this one event.

After closing her eyes and fidgeting, Eve groaned and

sat up, turning on the light. Reaching for a notebook and pen, she rearranged her pillows and started jotting down notes. Soon, she was out of bed putting the kettle on again and opening her laptop, surrounding herself with pieces of paper full of scribbles with ideas of events, memories of Stan and plans for the future.

Six

Eve groaned awkwardly as she woke. Pain ripped through her back and arms. She sighed to herself as she realised the position she was in, draped across the sofa, shivering gently, bent at an odd angle with one arm pinned behind her head. As she righted herself and sat up, paper fell off the sofa around her and she shot out a hand to save her empty mug from falling off the table. At least she'd finally managed to get some sleep. Blinking to clear her vision, Eve picked up the papers, trying to decipher the notes. Then she frowned. What was that noise? Something vibrating against wood.

Eyes wide, Eve cleared her table in one sweep and found her phone underneath a sheath of papers. She recognised the number immediately.

'Hello?' She held the phone away and coughed. 'Hello?' she repeated in a clearer voice.

'Eve? It's Jeff Hargreaves.'

Eve's heart began pounding.

'Hi,' she managed.

'Hi. Sorry, I know it's early. But I didn't know how much time you needed. We're good to go ahead with the ghost tour tonight. Erm…do you need anything from us? From me, I mean, I'll be the only one here. Along with Janine. Glen and Wendy have gone home. So it's just us. So, what do we do now? How does this work?'

Grinning, Eve silently punched the air and then took a second to regain her composure.

'That's wonderful news, thank you so much. You don't need to do anything. I'll need to come over early and set everything up, make sure everything and everyone's in place. Jan can help me, she already knows where everything goes.'

'Oh. Okay. I mean, I'd like to help, if I can. What did my dad used to do?'

A shot of pleasure twisted through Eve's gut.

'That would be great, if you don't mind. He'd help with the decorating where he could but mostly he was the ideas man. He'd sit back and boss us around and—' Eve paused, realising what she'd just said.

Jeff gave something of a sad laugh.

'Don't worry. This is your thing. I won't be doing any bossing around.'

'Thanks,' said Eve. 'I mean it. Thank you, for letting us go ahead. I know this is a really difficult time. Losing your dad at Christmas is bad enough without having me in your way. So I really appreciate you doing this.'

There was a long pause on the phone and Eve began to wonder if Jeff had gone. Had the connection cut out? She opened her mouth to see if he was still there when he spoke.

'I think it'll be fun,' he said and there was a slight crack in his voice that tore at Eve. 'Dad would have wanted it to go ahead.'

Eve nodded and then realised Jeff couldn't see her.

'Are you okay?' she said before clenching her eyes shut.

What a stupid thing to ask. 'I mean, you know, if you want to talk, about anything, I'm a fairly unbiased ear. I'm happy to listen.'

'That's very kind of you, to offer free therapy, but I'm all right.'

'Okay. Look,' continued Eve without thinking. 'If you need a break today or over Christmas in general, my friend owns a bakery on the high street. Flour Power Bakery. She does the best mince pies and cakes and coffee. And I'm often down there, so if you do ever fancy a chat.'

She could almost hear Jeff smiling.

'Thanks,' he said. 'I'll bear that in mind. So, what time will you be coming today?'

'I'll be there around two this afternoon. Is that okay? People start arriving after dark, around half five. We get going at six. It'll all be over by eight.'

'Wow. I can even have an early night.'

Eve laughed.

'That's the beauty of winter ghost tours.'

There was another pause and this time Eve waited.

'Be honest, are there really ghosts in this house?'

Eve hesitated, wondering how he would react to the truth.

'Honestly? I guess it depends on how you define ghosts.'

Jeff barked a laugh.

'Not sure I deserved the philosophical answer but thanks anyway. See you later.'

'See you. And thanks again.'

Jeff hung up and Eve lowered her phone, staring at the screen. Then she jumped up and screamed, 'Yes!' at the top of her voice, her arms in the air. Giggling, she danced into her bathroom and had a quick hot shower before pulling on layers of warm clothes, trapping in the heat, grabbing her bag and coat, and slamming the door behind her.

'It's on!' she yelled as she walked into Flour Power

Bakery. 'Beth?'

Beth appeared from below the counter, making Eve jump.

'Don't do that,' she said, hand over her heart as Beth grinned.

'It's not my fault that you walk in while I'm down there.'

'Really? Because sometimes it feels like you see me coming and you hide.'

Beth made a noise as if that couldn't possibly be true but that smile was still on her lips.

A couple sitting in the corner grinned at them as Eve undid her coat.

'What's on?' Beth asked. 'Coffee?'

'Please. I haven't had any breakfast. I fell asleep on my sofa last night while working. I know, I know,' she added when Beth gave her a look. 'I couldn't sleep. And they say you should get up and do something when you can't sleep.'

'Do something like read a book, not worry about your business,' said Beth. 'And then go back to bed when you're feeling sleepy.'

Eve waved her words away with exaggerated gestures.

'Whatever. I'll have a coffee, yes, thank you. And the ghost tour is on. Jeff called me this morning, woke me up in fact, and told me it's on. We're on!' Eve gave a little squeal and then was instantly distracted by the cakes in the display case by the till. 'You made sugar biscuits.'

'I did. First thing. They're fresh, I only just put them out, and no you can't have a sugar biscuit for breakfast. I'll make you some toast with eggs, if you like?'

'How about pancakes? Your pancakes are incredible.'

'Eggs on toast it is,' said Beth, placing Eve's coffee on the counter and disappearing into the kitchen. 'Grab a table,' she called over her shoulder.

Eve took one by the window. The bakery hadn't had a chance to steam up yet so she had a perfectly clear view of the high street, the cars moving past and the odd early morning shopper or person on their way to work.

Pete appeared from the kitchen and greeted Eve.

'I hear the ghost tour is back on?' he asked her, taking his place behind the till.

'It is.'

'Sort of wish I'd bought tickets now. Are you sold out?'

'Yeah. Sorry. I would say maybe next time but…' Eve shrugged.

'You'll find somewhere better,' he told her. 'You know, you should branch out. Offer your services elsewhere. What about that old medieval jail that's over there somewhere.' He pointed to his right. 'I'm always seeing signs for it but never been. A ghost tour in a medieval jail. Think about that.'

Eve did think about it, immediately her brain took the idea and began running through the possibilities. She'd never wanted to start a ghost tour business, she'd just enjoyed running events.

'Maybe,' she said as the door opened and a family of four came in, bringing a gust of cold air with them. 'Thanks. Good idea.'

Pete gave her a nod before turning his attention to the family. Eve went back to staring out of the window, sipping at her coffee. Maybe she could follow the ghost tour ideas, but that would probably mean believing a little more in the paranormal. Perhaps this was an opportunity to try something new. She narrowed her eyes as her mind whirred and then started as Beth placed a couple of plates piled with toast and poached eggs on the table. She sat opposite Eve and then stared at her friend.

'What? What are you thinking now?'

Eve realised she was looking suspiciously at Beth.

'You've always been a good cook,' she murmured.

Beth sat back.

'Yeah?' she said cautiously.

'Have you ever thought about cooking for dinner parties?'

'Yup.'

'And?'

'Nope.'

Eve sighed.

'Look, I know our passions can intertwine sometimes and that's wonderful,' said Beth, cutting into her toast and egg, the yolk spilling out. 'But that doesn't mean we should go into business together. We've talked about this.'

'Yeah, I know,' said Eve, picking up her knife and fork. 'But what if we weren't in business together? What if I hired you? To cater at parties. Ooh, at weddings!'

Beth watched her friend's animated features and smiled as she swallowed her mouthful.

'You want to become a wedding planner? That's quite a difference from murder mysteries and ghost hunts.'

'Yeah.' Eve pushed her egg and then sliced into it, watching the yolk run out in a glorious mess. 'You know what scares me?'

'What?'

'What if Stan had all the good ideas? What if, without him, I'm just good at organising where and when people should be without making the event actually good?'

Beth considered Eve as they tucked into the breakfasts.

'You learned a lot from Stan,' she said. 'And you had incredible ideas before he came into your life. Just imagine what you'll be capable of now.'

Eve's eyes filled up. She blinked the tears back, sniffed and filled her mouth with toast and runny egg.

The door to the bakery opened, sending another waft of cold air over them. Eve swallowed hard as Jeff walked in and approached the counter. He took off gloves as he talked to Pete.

'That's Jeff,' Eve hissed. Beth looked back over her shoulder just as Pete pointed them out to Jeff, who turned to look at them. Beth turned back sharply, raising her eyebrows at Eve.

'Cute,' she mouthed.

Eve gave her a warning look.

Jeff wandered over, his eyes on Eve.

'Hi. You decided to come check this place out?' Eve asked, smiling up at him.

'Yeah. Thought it might be good to get out.' Jeff looked around the bakery. 'When I was a kid, this was a haberdashery.'

'Ha! Yeah. It was when I bought it. The planning permission was fun, I can tell you,' said Beth. 'I'm Beth.' She held out a hand.

'Jeff Hargreaves.' Jeff shook her hand, glancing at Eve who was searching for the right words.

'Lovely to meet you. I'm so sorry about your father. He was a wonderful man. I always made extra mince pies for him. I used to sneak them to him when Eve and Jan weren't looking.'

Eve looked at her friend.

'Did you? I never knew that.'

'I'm very good at being sneaky,' said Beth. She stood up as Eve ate her last mouthful of breakfast. Beth took her plate. 'I'll let you two talk,' she said, giving Eve an encouraging look. Eve ignored her.

'I'm just getting a coffee to takeaway,' said Jeff.

'Pete'll bring it over when it's ready,' said Beth, gesturing to the chair she'd vacated.

Jeff sat down and they watched as Beth bustled into the kitchen at the back.

'She seems nice.'

'She's all right. I mostly stick around for the cake,' said Eve, smiling as Jeff looked at her. 'We've been friends since university,' she clarified with a shrug. 'Sometimes she knows me better than I know myself.' She stopped and considered those words, glancing up at Jeff with new eyes. He didn't notice. 'You don't recognise her? She grew up around here too. I only moved here about five years ago. There's only the one high school here, right?'

Jeff fidgeted and it took Eve a moment to recognise it as embarrassment.

'We were shipped off to private school. We didn't venture down here often. Sometimes, Mum would take me into the shops, but usually only around Christmas.' He breathed in and closed his eyes. 'I can smell mince pies.'

'It always smells of fresh mince pies in here, from November to the end of the year.'

Jeff and Eve looked into each other's eyes, both smiling. Just as it occurred to Eve that, while the silence wasn't awkward, perhaps someone should speak, Pete placed a takeaway cup of coffee down in front of Jeff.

'Thanks.' Jeff began to pull his gloves back on and a hint of panic flittered through Eve.

'So, erm, where do you live now?' she asked.

Jeff sat back.

'London. I run an architectural firm.'

'Really? You're an architect?'

'I am. I think that's why Dad wanted me to have the house. I think he thought I'd appreciate it more. Although I'm not sure how true that is.'

'You don't like the house?'

Jeff appeared shocked.

'No. I adore it. It's beautiful and old and home. It's just that both Wendy and Glen have families. Shouldn't a house like that be filled with warmth and laughter and children?'

Eve fought against a smile and distracted herself with the last of her coffee.

'Oh, I don't know. It sounds like a nice place for a fun uncle to live.'

Jeff laughed.

'And a nice place to start a family,' he murmured.

'Is that the plan?'

Jeff shrugged.

'It always was. I just can't seem to find anyone to start one with. Dating's hard. Don't you think?'

Eve nodded, trying to remember the last date she'd been on.

'I'm beginning to think that the right woman for me

doesn't live in London,' Jeff continued. 'I get the feeling I've been looking in the wrong places.'

'I know what you mean,' Eve murmured. Jeff looked up into her eyes. 'I mean, you get to a certain age and you have to start wondering if your dream man, or woman, even exists.'

Jeff grinned.

'What's the dream man then?'

Eve chose her next words carefully.

'The usual,' she said. 'Attractive, charming, intelligent, great sense of humour.'

'I think quite a few of them exist?'

'Yeah, but none have been quite right so far. Go on then, what's the dream woman?'

'Fun,' said Jeff. 'I want someone I can have fun with. Someone a bit different.'

Eve softened.

'Yeah. Someone that's just a touch quirky.'

'Exactly.'

'Who you can have in-jokes with but also serious conversations,' Eve added.

'Yes. Who likes hugging. I like hugging.'

'Me too. And staying in and watching a movie.'

'With popcorn.'

Eve and Jeff stopped and searched one another's eyes.

'Someone who likes Christmas,' Eve murmured.

'Someone who'll stay up and look at the stars, just in case,' Jeff added.

Eve's heart was pounding, her mouth dry, but she couldn't take her eyes from Jeff. He didn't move, his blue eyes soft, a smile playing on his lips.

The door to the bakery opened and this time the wind pushed the cold air in. Everyone in the bakery complained until the door was shut. Jeff shivered and pulled his coat tighter around his neck.

'I'd best be going,' he said, standing up and taking his coffee. 'See you this afternoon?'

'With bells on,' Eve murmured. Jeff glanced back to her curiously and she mentally shook herself. 'Two o'clock. See you then.'

.

Seven

'Merry Christmas Eve Eve!' Janine cried, leaving the house with open arms as Eve got out of the car. Eve grinned and let Stan's old housekeeper embrace her in a tight bear hug. Janine was approaching her late sixties and seemed to have an apron for every occasion. She was rarely straight faced and always a little flushed. Her silvery dark hair was usually tied back in a mess of a bun, mostly to keep it out of the food she prepared. Janine loved a clean house but she was the first to admit that she was at her happiest in a kitchen playing with and making something delicious. Her breads were quite famous amongst her friends and she'd even taught Beth a few things. Eve hugged her back, breathing in the scent of roast beef in her hair.

'You're cooking,' she said, her voice muffled by Janine's hair and coat.

'Indeed I am. Roast beef pastry parcels and festive sausage rolls. With vegan options.' Janine pulled away, her eyes brimming with tears and that was when Eve noticed how red the woman's eyes were. She took Janine's hand and squeezed it.

'I'm so sorry, Jan.'

Janine tried to smile but her chin quivered. The tears fell down her cheeks.

'Oh, blast.' Producing a crumpled tissue from her pocket, she wiped at her eyes. 'I thought I was done with this.'

'I don't think we'll be done with it for a while,' Eve told her. 'You need to let it out.'

Janine nodded.

'How are you holding up?' she asked.

Eve looked up at the house.

'Okay, I think. I don't think it'll hit me until after to-night. Hopefully not during tonight.'

Janine followed her gaze up to the house.

'I was so pleased that Jeff is letting you go through with the ghost hunt. It was always my favourite. Stan would have been happy about that. Although I can almost hear him chastising Jeff about not having the murder mystery, can't you? Anyway, the house is cleaned and some of the decorations are up. It's surprisingly difficult knowing where things go without Stan telling me what to do.' Janine sniffed. 'Do you want to take a look?'

Eve nodded and began to follow her into the house.

'What do you think of Jeff?' Janine whispered over her shoulder.

Eve sighed.

'He seems nice. Is he here?'

'Yes. He was sorting through boxes when I started decorating. He offered to help but he was more useless than I am. I think we both need some direction from you.' Janine held the door open for Eve and shut it behind them, gesturing to the grand staircase. 'He's up there. Shall we go find him? I know he'd love to help.'

Eve took a moment to breathe in the scents of the tall pine tree, the chill that comes from trying to heat such a large house, and the ever-present smell of polish. The delicious warm aromas of roasting beef and spices came through from the kitchen and Eve's stomach rumbled despite having just polished off a mini chocolate yule log made by Beth.

'Yes, let's get decorating,' she said, shrugging off her coat. Janine took it from her, snatching it when Eve went to protest.

'I'll put these away and come find you upstairs. You go find Jeff. He's probably in his father's study. I left the box of decorations with him. Lord only knows where he's put that large spider.' Janine walked away, humming to herself and Eve watched for a moment, wondering what the woman's plans were after Christmas was over. Maybe Eve could convince her to go into the party planning business as Beth wasn't keen.

Eve walked up the stairs, her hand trailing on the banister, watching the tree as she rose up until she could almost touch the angel on the top. She paused for a moment, feeling Stan's presence, and then continued on. The landing was bright and airy, certainly not good enough for a ghost tour. Eve checked in on the rooms that were used during the tour and left those doors open, closing the others, until she reached Stan's study. Inside, Jeff was sitting at his father's desk leafing through a book. She knocked gently on the door and Jeff looked up, smiling as his vision focused on her.

'Happy Christmas Eve Eve, Eve,' he said, grinning.

For a moment, Eve was taken aback.

'Sorry, I bet you get that all the time…at this time of year,' said Jeff, placing the book down on the desk. Eve didn't get a chance to correct him. He looked around, inhaling deeply. 'I always loved this room when I was little. Dad used to read in here with me. Some days I'd play with my Lego on the floor while he was working.'

'Oh? You were an architect from an early age then?'

Jeff lovingly caressed the arms of the chair he was

sitting on.

'According to Dad, I was always building something. Out of blocks, Lego, snow, sand, mashed potato.'

Eve smiled.

'This has always been my favourite room,' she murmured. 'There's something particularly cosy about it.'

'Especially with the fire lit,' Jeff agreed. 'I'm making this my own study and library, so it won't be changing. I'll just be adding more books.'

Eve blinked and looked away as Jeff caught her studying him.

'What would you do?' he asked. 'If this place was yours?'

Eve paused, wondering if she'd heard him right.

'You mean, if I was you?'

'No. If you were you but you'd inherited this place. What would you do with it? Would you live here?'

'Of course,' she said, without hesitation. Jeff smiled. Eve considered the rest of her response. 'I'd live here, but I'd also hold events here. But then, that's my business, isn't it. And I'd sell my friend's cakes and things here during the events. But it'd be a family home too, because that's what it should be. A home, filled with warmth and laughter and love. And cake,' she added.

Jeff watched her, still smiling.

'That sounds wonderful.'

'Really? Even the business part?'

Jeff nodded, glancing down at his father's desk.

'I guess I could move my firm up here. Or at least have another office here. I don't fancy splitting my time between here and London.'

Eve's shoulders dropped. So that was why he'd asked. He was trying to work out whether to live in the house or go back to London. Eve couldn't imagine not living in the Manor if you owned it.

'Jan said you might want to help with the decorating?' she asked.

'Oh, yes.' Jeff jumped up and walked around the desk. 'I had a go but didn't have a clue what to do. I thought I'd best leave it to the professional.'

'It just takes a bit of practise, that's all,' she told him as he fetched the box. 'We need to put up some cobwebs. Jan keeps this place too clean. And there's a giant spider. Where's the giant spider?'

'In the bedroom.' Jeff pushed past Eve and led her down the hallway, opening a door to the left where Eve hadn't checked yet. Inside was a double bed facing the wall and on top of the covers was a giant, furry black spider. 'I thought he needed a rest,' Jeff added.

Eve laughed.

'He was very busy a couple of months ago for Halloween,' she admitted, walking inside and picking the spider up. 'He goes on one of the doors, in the shadows. Stan managed to get him to move at the just right moment on Halloween and made a woman scream.'

Jeff grinned.

'Dad and his pranks.'

Eve began to unpack the box of decorations and walk Jeff through the ghost tour, telling him where to place the cobwebs and just how to position a witch in the corner, by the window. Janine came up to help and soon she was putting the finishing touches to the house as Eve instructed Jeff where to put the lights. It was dusk by the time they finished, the shadows growing longer around the house.

Jeff turned on the Christmas lights, alongside the glowing ghost tour ones, and began playing some low Christmas music as Eve welcomed Lyn the psychic.

'All done,' said Jeff, approaching Eve and Lyn.

'Great. Thanks. Jeff, this is Lyn, she leads the ghost tours.'

'Jeff,' said Lyn, taking his hand before he'd fully outstretched it and shaking it hard. 'I'm so sorry about your father. Stan was a wonderful man.'

'Thanks.' Jeff took his hand back. 'Do you run many

ghost tours?'

'Oh, yes.' Lyn held up her chin proudly. 'I mostly do séances and readings, but I do love a good ghost tour. I wonder what we'll find tonight. Perhaps Stan will come to say hello. Are those beef pastries I smell?' Lyn wandered off towards the kitchen and there came the raised voices of excited women as she found Janine.

'Well, that's it,' said Eve. 'Beth will arrive later with the mince pies and she and Jan will get the brass band into place. Just need the customers to arrive now. They'll come in dribs and drabs, so we'll need to make sure the food and drinks are ready.'

'They eat first?'

'We offer them the treats Jan's prepared along with a little glass of wine or juice when they arrive. Just until everyone's here and it's dark enough to start.'

Jeff nodded, distracted.

'Are you okay?' Eve asked. 'You don't have to stick around if you'd rather have some time alone. You know the route, so you can go and hide if you prefer?'

'Oh, no. No. I'd love to be involved. At least to follow on the tour, if that's okay?'

'Of course.' Eve resisted the urge to reach out to him, despite how much her instincts screamed at her to touch his arm comfortingly.

'I dreamt about him last night,' said Jeff after a moment, his voice low, his gaze on the Christmas tree.

'About your father?'

Jeff nodded.

'We were here, standing here, and he was happy.' Jeff smiled. 'I woke up and sobbed my eyes out.' He sighed.

This time Eve's instincts acted before she could stop them. She reached out and brushed her hand against his, taking it and squeezing. Jeff looked down at their hands and then up at her, his eyes rimmed red.

She smiled and went to take her hand away but Jeff held it tightly.

'I see now why you were important to him,' he murmured. 'Thank you, for bringing him all this joy, right up until the end.'

Eve's nose stung as her eyes filled.

Jeff dropped her hand quickly as there came a knock at the front door.

'Oh.' Eve wiped at her eyes. 'They're here. We're starting. Can you go tell Jan?'

Jeff left without saying anything and Eve turned to the front door, taking a deep breath. It was time to put away thoughts of grief and what should have been. There was a ghost tour to run.

Eight

Within half an hour, everyone had arrived and the Manor was filled with a warm glow, gentle chatter and laughter against the backdrop of the soft music. Lyn stepped forward and turned the music off before tapping on her glass with her long fingernails.

'Ladies and gentlemen!' She waited until the chatter had quietened and she had everyone's attention. 'We're about to begin. Please place your glasses on a table near you and gather at the bottom of the stairs.'

There was movement as the group did as they were told and Lyn positioned herself on the stairs. Eve found Jeff and, giving him a warm smile, positioned them so that they took up the rear of the group. Janine turned off some of the lights, creating a stir of murmurs in the group. Jeff flinched, looking around the hall. He took a shuddering breath as Lyn began.

'This manor house was built in the late eighteenth century but it stands on the foundations of something much older. Records show that this land once belonged to a monastery and the remains of a chapel have been found in the grounds. Naturally there are tales of spirits of the monks who once called that monastery home being spotted in the grounds, mostly going about their duties but sometimes watching those pottering about the gardens. We'll talk more about them later, when we head outside.

'Since the manor house was built upon the land sold by the church, a number of families have lived here. As with all families, there have been a fair share of secrets and scandal, leading up to the current owners, the Hargreaves family, the patriarch of which sadly passed away only days ago. Stanley Hargreaves loved these tours.' Lyn paused to close her eyes. 'I am sure you will all join me in sending our love and deepest sympathies to his family and friends who have lost a wonderful man. And we reach out to Stanley, if he is still among us, to invite him to join us on this tour tonight. Just for once, to become part of that which he enjoyed so much.'

Eve glanced up at Jeff, unsure whether Lyn's words were in poor taste or not. Jeff didn't react, keeping his eyes on Lyn. Eve looked back to the stairs, wondering if she would catch the outline of Stan on the steps behind Lyn. There was nothing there but shadows.

Lyn spoke a little more of what to expect, building the tension further, before asking the group to follow her up the stairs.

The group moved silently and Eve fell into old habits, watching those in front of her peering into the shadows, making each other jump as they brushed shoulders and laughing nervously. Lyn's voice faded as Eve watched the group enjoying themselves, until Jeff flinched, catching Eve's attention.

'This bedroom was also the room belonging to a young woman who fell madly in love with a wealthy man from the city. He promised to marry her and their ceremony was arranged in the local church for Christmas Eve. On the day of the wedding, our young bride put on her gown and travelled excitedly to meet her groom surrounded by family and friends. The groom never turned up. Thinking he had fallen out of love with her, she ran all the way back to this house and shut herself away in her room. She refused to eat or drink, she wouldn't speak to anyone or let anyone into the room. She died of a broken heart surrounded by these four walls, her door locked from the inside. Her groom-to-be, however, died on his way to his wedding when the horses pulling his carriage spooked on a bridge, the carriage capsizing and throwing our young groom into the water where he drowned. You might hope that their spirits would meet in the afterlife, but every Christmas weeping can be heard from this empty room, as our young bride returns to mourn what could have been.'

The group silently appraised the bedroom and then followed Lyn further down the hallway.

'Is that true? I don't remember that story,' Jeff whispered.

Eve only gave him a smile and followed the group, unaware that Jeff was no longer behind her.

It was only when Jeff had caught her up that she noticed he'd been missing for those few seconds. She took his arm, trying to gauge how he was feeling.

There was a scream as a motion sensitive light flicked on, illuminating the giant spider on the next door. Eve resisted the urge to cackle. Jeff started, his hand gripping Eve's arm and pulling her back. She glanced up to him as his nerves calmed.

'You put that there,' she murmured. 'Remember?'

Jeff gave a nervous laugh.

'This room leads up to the attic, long since locked and never reopened. Beyond the door is where it is rumoured a witch once lived, casting spells over those who lived in the town, granting them one Christmas wish each. But each wish came with a cost. So it was that one cold December evening, someone came to knock on her door.'

Eve nearly yelped when a grip closed on her wrist and pulled her back. She looked up into Jeff's eyes, his skin paling.

'Are you okay?' She frowned, concern etched into her features as she studied him. 'You don't look okay. Is this too much?'

'Are they real?' he asked, speaking too fast. 'The ghost stories. About this place?' he hissed.

Eve looked back to the group to make sure they couldn't hear her and then led Jeff away, back towards the stairs, just in case.

'No,' she told him. 'I mean, that woman did exist and her groom did die on the way to the wedding, but she knew and she mourned, and went on to marry someone else. I think she was from the first family to live here. The family that built this house. We adapted it and added the bit about the Christmas wedding. And there was never a witch who lived in the attic granting Christmas wishes for an awful cost until her true love came back for her one Christmas. That one was your dad's idea. There was a chapel and monastery here though. Those stories are reportedly true but I've personally never seen anything and neither did your dad.'

Jeff exhaled long and deep.

'So, this house isn't haunted?'

'No. Lyn just tells a good story. I'm sorry. This was a bad idea. I shouldn't have let you tag along. I should have known it might freak you out. Come on, let's go downstairs and chat with Jan over a mince pie. See if Beth's here with the band.' Eve went to go down the stairs.

'Only, I saw my dad.'

Eve stopped and turned back to Jeff.

'Excuse me?'

'In the bedroom. When everyone else had carried on. He stood in front of me and he smiled and then he looked at you. He looked…at peace…' Jeff's eyes glistened with unspent tears. 'Do you think I'm crazy?'

Eve was silent for a moment, her mouth open.

'Of course not,' she murmured, searching for the right comforting words. 'Lots of people say that they sense their loved ones after they've passed on. Maybe he came to say goodbye.'

Jeff nodded and rubbed at his eyes with a thumb.

The tour was coming back down the hallway, heading for the stairs and outside to continue the ghost stories out in the gardens. Eve and Jeff stood to the side and let them pass. The group was quiet but in the dim light, Eve could make out the smirks and sparkling eyes. She exhaled slowly. They were having a good time. At least there was that.

Once the group had passed, Eve turned back to Jeff. He appeared thoughtful, then he strode past her, opening the door to his father's study and wandering inside, behind the desk to the window. Eve followed slowly.

'Do you believe in ghosts?' he asked, his back to Eve.

'I believe in something,' she admitted. 'But I'm not quite sure what.'

'What if Dad is haunting the house?' Jeff asked quietly.

'Would that be a bad thing?' Eve mused, stepping further into the study and wondering if she could turn the lights on. The shadows flickered from the spooky lights placed in the hallway and the emotion coming off Jeff in waves was making her see things that weren't there. A lengthening shadow, a flash of light that couldn't exist, the door moving ever so slightly on its own.

'It would mean he had unfinished business, wouldn't it.' Jeff turned to look at her, his cheeks wet with tears.

All thoughts of shadows and doors moving went out of Eve's head and she walked over to Jeff, using her sleeve over her thumb to wipe his tears away.

'Your father was a happy man,' she told him in a loud voice to dispel the mood. 'He was loved and he loved. He had fun and he ate what he wanted and he said things how he saw them. What business could he possibly have left unfinished?'

Jeff nodded, his brows knitting into a frown as he thought.

'Apart from turning this into a real ghost tour,' he suggested with a weak attempt at a laugh. A chill ran through Eve and she echoed the laugh.

'Nah. He wouldn't do that. He knew ghosts terrified me. He liked a prank and spooking people but actually scaring them? No. Did you feel scared when you saw him?'

'No,' Jeff admitted. 'Although…' He looked into Eve's eyes. 'There was something strange about the way he looked after you as you walked away.'

'Oh, don't say that,' said Eve, wrapping her arms around herself.

'He looked at you with love but also…'

'Also?' Eve encouraged, wondering how on earth Jeff would finish that sentence.

Jeff searched her eyes again, his own softening, and then, infuriatingly, he shrugged.

'I don't know. It doesn't matter. Come on. They're outside now, let's go join them.' Jeff walked away, out of the room and Eve listened to his thumping footsteps on the stairs. She remained behind Stan's desk in his study, unable to move, wondering what had just happened.

She glanced about the dark room.

'Stan?' she said, loud enough that she was sure all the shadows could hear her. 'If you're there, if you can hear me, please don't haunt this house. Please be at peace. And what was Jeff trying to say?' she added quietly to herself.

There came a bang and Eve squealed, her heart pounding. Her hand automatically going to her chest to calm herself, she carefully made her way across the room where a framed photo had fallen from the wall. Gingerly, she picked up the photo. It was black and white showing Stan posing with his wife, his arm around her waist, grinning like a man who had everything he needed in the world. They weren't as young as Eve had expected. Stan was perhaps in his late thirties although his wife could have been in her late twenties. She appeared giddy, her smile broad and her cheeks flushed. Eve couldn't help but smile back at them, feeling the love coming off the photo.

'You're with her now, aren't you? I hope you are,' she murmured. Turning the picture over so she could see how to hang it back up, Eve stopped. On the back of the frame, written in large letters with what looked like a fine marker pen, were the words, *Everything You Need Is Right In Front Of You*.

A sob wrenched through Eve, surprising her. With trembling hands, holding back the tears, she hung the photo back up and smiled again at Stan and his wife.

'I hope one day I'm as happy and in love as you were,' she told him. 'I miss you so much already. Thank you for passing your fun gene onto your son,' she added, thinking of Jeff's smile and the twinkle in his eyes.

As she turned to leave, there was another thump. Eve slowly turned back to face the room, terrified that she would come face to face with Stan's spirit.

No. It was another framed photo falling from the wall. Frowning, Eve picked it up and glanced at the picture. There were no words on the back this time but the photo was of Stan's three children. Glen, standing tall and proud over his siblings, Wendy grinning stupidly for the camera, and young Jeff, sticking his tongue out. Eve grinned in a half laugh, hanging the picture back up and pausing to stare at the young Jeff. The resemblance to his father was uncanny, even from such an early age. Her gaze lingered as her body turned and she left the room, heading towards the stairs, the smile still on her lips.

Nine

Eve walked out into the chill of the dark evening and joined the end of the tour group as they wandered past. Jeff was trailing behind, a thoughtful expression in his eyes and brow. Eve's stomach twisted as she caught sight of him. It made her hesitate as the tingles spread through her body but then Jeff caught sight of her and she didn't have the time to work out what those feelings meant.

'There you are.' He waited for her as the group headed towards the orchard. 'Where did you go?'

'I was still in the study. Something weird happened,' said Eve, catching him up.

'Oh?'

'A photo fell off the wall. Of your mum and dad. Stan had written a message on the back.'

Jeff stopped walking and stared at her.

'What did it say?'

'Everything you need is right in front of you,' Eve quoted. 'Very romantic. He really did love your mum.

Whenever he would talk about her, I would wish that I'd find someone one day who loved me as much as he loved her.'

Jeff smiled.

'Yeah. Well. You didn't live with them. Kissing and cuddling all the time. It was disgusting.'

Eve laughed.

'Really? You don't want that?'

Jeff's gaze lingered on her and Eve's stomach flipped again.

'Oh, definitely. I just didn't want that when I was a kid. It was embarrassing back then. Now I'm proud of them for being that affectionate with each other.' He looked past Eve and up at the house behind her. 'Everything you need is right in front of you,' he murmured.

Eve followed his eyes to the house.

'Do you think that's true?' When she turned back, she reeled to find Jeff staring intently at her.

'I do,' he murmured, his gaze travelling down her body before he sharply turned and strode to catch up with the tour group.

Breathing hard, Eve followed at a slower pace to give herself some time to think. If she didn't know better, she could have sworn that Jeff was attracted to her. She'd been wrong about these things in the past, so it probably meant nothing, especially as he was grieving his father. Given her own physical reactions, did she find Jeff attractive?

She studied him as she caught up, moving to stand beside him at the entrance to the small orchard. It was a square patch of land planted with apple and pear trees, enclosed by hedge and an open fence to allow wildlife in and out. Of all the grounds, this was Eve's favourite. It was also the favourite spot of the local bat population who swooped around the trees at dusk before the insects gravitated towards what light emanated from the house.

Now, the orchard was festooned with twinkling fairy lights. There was a rose arch wrapped in lights at the end of the orchard and around it were the brass band. As Lyn finished her talk and pointed out the table of warm mince pies, gingerbread ghosts and mulled wine off to the side, the band struck up with a gentle rendition of Silent Night.

Eve inhaled slowly. The air was heavy, filled with the scent of mud, bare trees, an open sky and the waft of the wine, pies and gingerbread. If she wasn't mistaken, the scent of snow hung in the air, bringing up wonderful cosy childhood memories. It was only then that Eve realised she'd forgotten to grab her coat on the way out. She hugged herself, giving a little shiver. Then, without warning, her shoulders were warm. She looked up to find Jeff placing his coat around her.

'What idiot comes out here on Christmas Eve Eve without a coat,' he chastised gently, his eyes twinkling in the fairy lights. Eve's breath caught in her throat.

'Won't you be cold?'

Jeff shrugged.

'I'll let you know when I am and you can give it me back.' He gave her a wink and then walked over to the mince pies.

Eve suppressed an involuntary giggle at the wink and watched him go. Over his shoulder, Beth caught her eye. There was no way Jeff wouldn't have seen the look on Beth's face and Eve's pulse raced at the thought.

'That went very well, I think. A couple of people have already been over to ask me questions,' said Lyn at Eve's shoulder. Eve nodded, not taking her eyes from Jeff's back. 'It's such a shame it'll be our last one.'

With those words, Eve deflated, her attention ripped from Jeff and onto Lyn.

'It is, isn't it,' she murmured.

'Stan would have loved this,' said Lyn, eyeing Eve, a strange smile on her face. 'Did he speak to you?'

Eve frowned.

'Jeff? Of course he did.'

'No. Stan. In the house. Did he speak to you just now?

I noticed you didn't come out into the garden with us.'

Eve stared at the woman, her jaw slowly dropping as the smile on Lyn's face grew.

'How did you—'

'I know you think you don't believe, love,' said the medium. 'I know you think I'm a fake,' she whispered so the customers wouldn't hear. 'But sometimes we think things, we believe things, to protect ourselves. Sometimes it can do you good to open your mind and explore the possibility of the thing that scares you being true. What does your gut tell you?'

Eve placed a hand over her gut as the fear swirled around.

'That Stan was trying to tell me something.'

Lyn gave a nod.

'And what does your gut think he was trying to tell you?'

Eve went to answer and then shook her head and shrugged.

'I have no idea.'

'Yes, you do. You have a good idea. What's the first idea that came to you? The message that Stan is trying to tell you. What's the message that you can't stop thinking about?'

Eve looked back to Jeff, now in conversation with Beth as he ate a mince pie. Lyn followed her gaze.

'Your gut is always right, Eve. And there's nothing to be scared of. Stan is happy and at peace. He told me so, in the hallway outside his study, as he watched you and his son talking.'

Lyn patted Eve on the arm and then walked a few steps away before a couple from the tour group approached her, asking excitedly about one of the ghost stories she'd told.

Eve kept her gaze on Jeff and then slowly wandered over.

Beth was laughing at something Jeff had said and she handed Eve a mince pie as she asked him, 'So, have you enjoyed the ghost tour?'

66

'I have. It's actually quite magical here, isn't it,' said Jeff, looking around the orchard as the brass band ended one song and started another. 'What do you do here for Halloween?'

'We put scary monsters in the trees and last year we did some bat detecting too. If they're around in October, they tend to be attracted to the orchard later at night as the lights attract all the flying insects,' said Eve. 'It's not magical but it's just as much fun. To be honest, I prefer Christmas.'

'I don't know. I like the cider we serve at Halloween,' said Beth. 'I prefer cider to mulled wine.'

'Me too,' Jeff agreed.

'And there's apple bobbing,' Eve added, looking around the orchard, picturing where everything would go. 'And pumpkins. Beth carves them. She's a woman of many talents.'

Beth shrugged.

'I just do what you tell me.'

Jeff smiled at Eve.

'I thought you said most of the ideas were Dad's?'

Eve considered that.

'Well, we use a lot of his ideas. The big spider was his idea. He bought that. You should keep it. I'll leave it here when we pack up.'

Jeff's expression fell.

'Yeah. I still need to talk to my sister about that.' He gave a little shiver and picked up a glass of mulled wine.

'You're cold. Here, take your coat back. I'll run back to the house and get mine.'

'No, no. I'm fine. My coat suits you,' said Jeff, taking the opportunity to look Eve up and down. Eve smiled and, behind Jeff, Beth smirked.

After a moment, Lyn caught Eve's eye before turning back to the group of women she was talking to.

'Oh, I hate to ruin the moment,' Eve said to Jeff and Beth. 'But Lyn basically just told me she's a real medium and that she also spoke to Stan upstairs.'

Jeff stared at her wide-eyed, lowering his hand holding his mulled wine. Beth frowned.

'What do you mean "also spoke to Stan"?' She looked between Jeff and Eve.

'A couple of photos fell off the wall while I was in the study, before I came out here,' Eve explained.

'A couple? I thought it was just the one, of Mum and Dad, with the message.'

'Message?' asked Beth.

'Yeah. "Everything you need is right in front of you". On the back of a picture of Stan with his wife, his arm around her, they both looked so happy. It's a lovely photo.'

'What was the other picture to fall down?' Jeff asked.

'The one of you,' said Eve and then added quickly, 'and your brother and sister.'

Jeff and Eve stared at each other for a moment.

'I saw Dad in one of the bedrooms,' Jeff told Beth in a quiet voice, his eyes still on Eve. 'He smiled at me, he was happy, and then he looked at Eve.'

Beth raised an eyebrow.

'Sounds to me an awful lot like your dad wanted the two of you to meet. Didn't you say Stan had invited you to Boxing Day dinner this year, Eve?'

Jeff raised an eyebrow.

'Did he?'

Eve blinked rapidly, pulling herself out of Jeff's gaze.

'He does every year,' she murmured. 'I spend Christmas with my parents so I've never been able to make it.' She sighed. 'I wish I had. Just once. I kept meaning to. This year was going to be the year. But then, I never wanted to be the odd one out or intrude. You know, it's a family time.'

'But you were family,' Beth prompted.

'That's what our Boxing Day is,' Jeff agreed. 'Jan comes too, and Harry and Dave who look after the garden. Last year a couple of cousins came with their kids. There were loads of us. It wouldn't have been awkward at all.'

'Oh. Well, now I really regret not going,' said Eve, looking down at her hands, her chest feeling so empty it hurt. How was this possible? To swing from feeling so full of emotion to so empty that the pain was almost too much.

'Don't be silly,' said Jeff. 'We all have our Christmas traditions and you spend yours with your parents. Dad should have invited them too if he really wanted you to come.'

'True,' said Eve, picturing it with a smile. 'That would have been nice. That didn't even cross my mind.'

Jeff took another glass of mulled wine.

'See, you're cold,' Eve pointed out as he cupped his hands around the warm glass. 'Here, take your coat and I'll go get mine.' She took his coat off her shoulders before he could argue. Beth handed her a glass of mulled wine to keep her warm on the walk over and while she was about it, Eve took a gingerbread ghost as well. The piles of treats were getting smaller by the minute and she wasn't going to be the one to miss out.

'At least let me come with you, then,' said Jeff, reluctantly taking his coat and then realising both of Eve's hands were full so he couldn't hand it back. He hesitated, as if about to drape it back across her shoulders but Eve moved too fast.

'Okay. Just in case something jumps out at me.' She flashed him a grin and bit off the tail of the gingerbread ghost. Beth smiled to herself, watching Jeff and Eve walk out of the orchard and away from the lights, chatter and music.

Ten

The house was dark, other than the sparkling lights of the Christmas tree, and full of echoes as Eve opened the front door and made her way to the coat room. Jeff followed closely, giving another shiver.

'I know the heating's on but we really should get the fire going.'

'The tour group will start going home soon,' Eve explained, pulling her coat on. 'I'll help Beth tidy up out there. You can get the fire going then. Do you want me to take the tour decorations down tonight? I should really, as tomorrow is Christmas Eve.'

'What? Oh no,' said Jeff. 'You can't do it tonight, it's too late.'

'It's still quite early. There'll be plenty of time. Unless you'd like to get settled, in which case I'm happy to come back tomorrow morning. I just thought you might want all of the cobwebs and things taken down before Christmas Eve.' Eve looked up at the large tree thoughtfully, although from the corner of her eye she could see Jeff staring at her.

'Okay,' he said carefully. 'I'll help you take them down tonight. It won't take long. And then you should stay. You've worked so hard today. Sit by the fire and have dinner with me and Jan. Beth can stay too. It'll be nice.'

Eve smiled.

'That does sound lovely. Thank you. If you're sure.'

'Of course,' said Jeff with a nod. 'Absolutely.'

'What are your Christmas plans?' Eve asked. 'What will you do?'

Jeff sighed, looking around the room.

'I think we'll still have it here. Wendy will bring her family and I think Glen's got his son this year. He better do, everything considered. Wendy usually cooks because she enjoys it for some reason and her roast potatoes are to die for. And then Boxing Day.' He glanced at Eve. 'Dad's invitation still stands. You're more than welcome to join us.'

Eve nodded.

'Thank you. I'll do that, if that's okay. Better late than never, right?'

Jeff gave a sad smile.

'Your parents can come too.'

'No. No, they'll understand. I should have come to Boxing Day here a long time ago. Will it just be you and Wendy and Glen though?'

'And Wendy's husband, that'll be awkward, they're not on the best terms right now, so you can save me from that.'

The corner of Eve's mouth lifted up as she watched Jeff think.

'And their children, of course,' he continued. 'Glen and his son. Jan'll be there and Harry and Dave. We've invited the cousins but I'm not sure if they'll come. I think we'll invite some of Dad's friends from the town. It might turn into a little night of remembering Dad.'

'Then I'm definitely coming,' said Eve, giving him what she hoped was a comforting smile. 'You hear that, Stan? I'll be here for Boxing Day,' she called into the house. 'And I hope you'll forgive me for all the times I didn't make it.'

There came no response, which Eve was glad of. She wasn't sure what she'd have done if a light had flickered or another picture had fallen or if they'd heard a voice.

They both jumped as excited gasps and cheers came from outside and both Jeff and Eve turned to the front door.

'What's going on?' Jeff walked to the door and peered out before laughing. Eve followed closely and then gave an excited squeal, pushing past Jeff onto the porch, lit up by fairy lights, to hold out her hand and catch the falling snowflakes.

'It's snowing!' she cried and there were cheers from the orchard in response. Eve laughed, stepping out among the flakes and twirling in her coat. Jeff watched from the porch, grinning. Eve wrapped her coat about her tighter and stepped back into the glow of the porch to watch the snow fall.

'Do you think people will have trouble leaving?' she asked after a moment.

'I doubt it. It's not falling that hard. Not yet,' Jeff said quietly.

'I guess I might have trouble leaving,' Eve murmured, before adding, 'Don't want to get snowed in.'

'Don't you?'

Eve glanced at Jeff to find him just behind her shoulder, gazing at her with soft eyes.

'Look up,' he murmured in her ear.

Her eyes flicked to above their heads and the sprig of mistletoe hanging there. She smiled at Stan's favourite Christmas touch. Then her gaze fell back down to Jeff as he moved closer to her. Her heart racing, she turned to face him, lifting her chin to him, wondering for a moment what to do with her hands.

His lips touched hers in a kiss. He was so warm and his lips so soft. In the background, the brass band began to play We Wish You A Merry Christmas. The tour was finished, the group would be filing back to the front of the house soon. They'd be caught kissing under the mistletoe. Eve considered pulling away but Jeff's hand snaked around her waist, pulling her closer. His lips tasted of the mulled wine and his cologne found its way up her nose. In that moment, she wanted nothing more than to snuggle into his arms and hold him close. The kiss broke but they didn't move apart. Instead, Jeff touched the tip of her nose with his and then pressed his forehead into hers, smiling.

'You know, when you said Dad's message was "everything you need is right in front of you", my second thought was the house. I want to live here properly, make it my home, leave London behind.'

'What was your first thought?' Eve asked breathlessly, looking up into his eyes, the blue twinkling in the low light.

'You,' he said, leaning down and kissing her again. Eve reached up and wrapped her arms around his neck, holding him close. She went up on tiptoe to get closer and he smiled into the kiss.

They broke apart to the sound of applause and found the entire tour group standing on the driveway before them. Squinting in sudden light, both Eve and Jeff looked behind them into the house. The lights had come on, not only in the hallway but in the rooms coming off the hallway.

'Did you do that?' Beth asked Janine, standing to the side of the group close to the porch.

'Not me,' came Janine's voice.

'I think Dad did it,' Jeff murmured, pulling Eve close and wrapping his arms around her in a hug. She did the same, putting her arms around him and resting her head on his chest, breathing in his scent.

From the front of the tour group, Lyn clapped her hands once with glee.

'Come on then!' shouted Beth. 'It's still snowing out here and it's freezing. Stop canoodling and get out of the way.'

Grinning, Jeff led Eve into the house and turned off the main lights, letting the fairy lights of the Christmas tree and around the porch light the way of the others. He kept an arm around Eve, as if she was planning on going anywhere else. She looked up at him until she caught his eye.

'Wanna stay for dinner, Beth?' Jeff asked, his gaze lingering on Eve.

'You sure you two don't want to be alone?' Beth asked.

'Plenty of time for that,' Eve murmured.

Jeff grinned as Beth playfully threw a gingerbread ghost at Eve.

***

Acknowledgements

A massive thank you to my mum, the avid romance
reader and my endless supporter.
Thank you also to the readers of my fantasy series,
Murray And Tidswell Paranormal Investigations, who
suggested that I leave some of the fantasy behind to
focus on the romance.

And a sweet thank you to Vicky of Tallulah's Bakery for
being not just a friend but the Queen of Sugar Biscuits.

Turn the page for a sneak peak
of the next book in the series.

That's It In
A Nutcracker

Available now from www.nicebycandlelight.co.uk

One

Beth's teeth ached by the time she pulled the car to a stop. Pulling up the handbrake, she took a deep breath, released her jaw muscles and centred herself. This was the part she hated. Every bump in the road had been agony, every turning had been with bated breath. Beth geared herself up and stepped out of her car, slamming the door behind her. Tentatively, she opened the boot and took away the cardboard walls she'd erected, along with the polystyrene padding and bubble wrap. Gradually, the tiers of the white wedding cake were revealed and Beth sighed in relief at the sight of them safe and sound. Leaving the cake where it was and locking her car, Beth went in search of the wedding planner. Through the grand entrance of the hotel, decorated beautifully with ivy and holly, and straight up to reception. They found the wedding planner who introduced himself as Simon and then helped Beth carry the cake tiers, stand and props into the main reception room.

'There's something wonderful about a Christmas wedding,' said Beth as she started putting the cake together. Simon stood over her, hands on his hips, eyes distant.

'Yeah.'

Beth glanced up at him.

'Everything okay?'

The wedding planner blinked and looked down to Beth.

'Yes, yeah. Sorry. This one's been a bit stressful.' He sighed. 'They're all stressful but the Christmas ones more so.' His eyes grew distant again. 'I never used to find them this bad.'

Beth waited but when he didn't continue, she turned back to the cake. The tiers were in place and she carefully added the white roses, a cascade of iced snow and a dusting of edible gold. Simon focused and grinned.

'That's beautiful.'

'Thank you.' Beth reached into her box of tricks and pulled out a business card that had been languishing there since she'd ordered them. The pile was getting low but it wasn't quite time to order more yet. 'Do you want my card? In case you have any other weddings down this way in the future? Flour Power Bakery. I'm on the high street.'

Simon took the card with some reluctance.

'Thanks but, to be honest, this might be my last wedding.'

'Oh? How come?'

'Sort of sick of organising weddings for other people,' Simon mumbled.

Beth did a double take at him.

'I get that,' she murmured. 'Always the baker, never the bride.' She gave a shrug. 'My friend's an event planner, if you ever want to hand anything over to someone else. I'd be happy to put you in touch. She's been talking about organising weddings. Keeps asking me to go into business with her.'

The wedding planner gave Beth a look.

'Why haven't you agreed?'

Beth gave the cake a final flourish and stepped back.

'Because I know how stressful wedding planning can be. You're not the first wedding planner I've met.'

Simon laughed and then checked the time.

'Speaking of which,' he murmured.

'Are you local?'

'No, I'm based in London. But the bride is from around here and this is a lovely venue.'

Beth nodded.

'If you fancy coming back out this way, my friend is organising a Christmas fair and baking competition this year. She used to do tours up at the Manor – that big house on the hill? – but the owner passed away a year ago. So no more tours, but the bakery competition and fair entry is for charity. Everyone's welcome. If you want to meet her or just fancy taking some time out shopping, getting in the Christmas mood, you should come along.'

'Are you entering the competition?'

Beth smiled.

'No, I can't. I've been asked to judge, but I'll have a stall so there'll be some of my stuff available. It's all for a good cause. All the proceeds, and I mean nearly every penny as none of us are getting paid for it and we're getting the venue for free, so everything's going to a homeless charity. The old man who used to own the Manor left it to his youngest son, it's a charity close to his heart.'

Simon raised an impressed eyebrow.

'How did your friend get the venue for free? Out of the goodness of his heart?'

Beth barked a laugh and crossed her arms, giving the cake one last going over with her sharp eyes.

'You could say that. They got together last Christmas and they're both smitten. She moved in a few months ago. He couldn't say no to her running an event from their home at Christmas and she couldn't say no to his choice of charity.'

Simon gave a deep sigh.

'Lucky them.'

Beth's smile faded.

'Yeah.'

A silence fell over them until the wedding planner's phone beeped.

'That's the bride. I best go. Thank you so much for the

cake, it's beautiful. And maybe I will check out this charity event of your friend's. If nothing else, it's a trip out of the city.'

Beth gave him a smile.

'I hope the wedding goes well.'

'Me too,' said Simon with a laugh before turning away and almost running out of the room. Beth made her exit at a slower amble, enjoying the twinkling fairy lights decorating the room and the tall Christmas tree in the corner. Wandering through the bar, she became distracted by the soft Christmas carols playing over the chatter as she weaved through the wedding guests arriving. Turning into reception, she gave a gentle *oof* and looked up into familiar brown eyes.

'Sorry,' she said automatically.

He took a second longer, recognition lighting up his features as he smiled and then apologised.

'I didn't know you knew the bride or groom?' Glen Hargreaves asked, his gaze flitting over Beth in her floury jeans and baseball cap, her coat covering the mess beneath. He frowned and met her eyes again.

'Oh yes, I come to every wedding like this. I never want to upstage the bride,' said Beth with a grin, holding out her arms to give him a better view of her outfit. As his frown deepened, she gave a chuckle. 'I'm just delivering the wedding cake,' she explained.

Glen's frown vanished, replaced with a smile.

'Oh, of course. Wonderful. I can't wait to taste it.'

There was a tantalising moment as they stared at one another, Beth frantically trying to work out what a normal person in a normal situation would say next.

'Are you friends with the bride or groom?'

'The groom, strangely,' said Glen, glancing behind her into the bar.

'Strangely?' asked Beth. 'How strange?'

Glen's eyes met hers again and this time they softened. Something shifted inside Beth.

'I worked with him once in London but she's the one from round here, although we hadn't met before. Small world, huh?'

'Yeah. Small world.' Beth caught herself looking at his lips and ripped her gaze back to his eyes. She opened her mouth to say more when a slender arm snaked its way around Glen's arm. It belonged to a tall, equally slender woman with long brown hair so thick that it belonged in a shampoo advert. She was wearing a low cut blue dress that brought out her eyes and Beth became acutely aware that she was wearing a baseball cap at a wedding.

Glen looked down at the woman and gave a small smile. There was a pause as the women looked at one another and then questioningly up at him.

'Beth, this is Joy. Joy, this is Beth. She's the wedding cake baker and friends with Eve.'

'Eve?' asked Joy, holding out her hand for Beth to take.

'Jeff's girlfriend. My brother?'

Joy gave an elegant singular nod and turned back to Beth.

'Pleasure to meet you.'

'And you,' said Beth with a dry mouth. She dropped Joy's limp hand. 'Well, I best be going. Can't be bringing down the wedding party looking like this. Have fun.' Without looking back she scrambled around Glen and Joy, heading for the door.

'Wait.'

Beth stopped but didn't turn back immediately. First, she scrunched her eyes closed as every fibre in her body told her to run as fast as she could for her car. Slowly, she pivoted on her trainer heel to look back up into Glen's eyes.

'Fancy a drink?'

Beth glanced to Joy who was checking her reflection in a mirror on the reception wall.

'Oh, thank you, but I don't want to interrupt or interfere or…anything.' Beth stepped back, closer to the door.

'No, no, you won't be. Joy, your friend's here, isn't she?'

Joy nodded.

'Over in the corner.' She waved to someone Beth couldn't see. 'If you don't mind?'

'Of course not,' said Glen, turning back to Beth. 'So, let me buy you a drink. Just one. We've got time before the ceremony starts.'

Beth looked down at herself. She used to dress up for delivering wedding cakes and each time she'd drop off the cake and make it back to her car without seeing anyone but the venue staff and perhaps a wedding planner or one family member making themselves useful. It had been a waste of makeup and fancy dresses. It was never part of the plan to bump into someone she knew on her way out and be asked to stay for a drink.

'Sure. Okay. A small one. And I'm driving so no alcohol.'

A grin broke out across Glen's face.

'Of course. C'mon.' He led the way to the bar and after a moment Beth followed, dragging her trainers into the room filled with dressed up wedding guests.

**

Printed in Great Britain
by Amazon